SUN FORGED

BOOK 3 OF THE GIFTING

Also by Sevannah Storm

The Blood of Legends Series
The Huntress
The Healer
The Gifting Series
Soul Forged
Fate Forged
Sun Forged
War Forged
Star Forged
Shadow Forged
Earth Forged
Lust Forged
Standalones
Xiaxan Fox
Ire of Silver
The Shikari
Sol Survivor
Plump Playwright Series
Plump Jane
Seducing Amelia
Loving Finley
Keeping Tessa
Kissing Navy

COMING SOON

Inkoded

Fire Forged

The Crucible of the Eternal

Acknowledgments

To L.A. Myles.

Lesley, you're the best. I'm so grateful to have you in my life. Thanks for being there for me, L. I couldn't have released this book and many others without you.

Hugsies.

CONTENTS

 Prologue

Earth
The oldest street in West Haven
Year of 2242, August

Ava cowered under the stern gaze of her foster mother, Mrs. Wheeler. She curled her butter-coated fingers into fists, trying not to wince. Seven-year-old Ruby, too mature for her age, gave the slightest shake of her head. Beside her, unaware of the tension in the stylish kitchen sat five-year-old Saira, stuffing her face with the food Ava had shared—a house rule she'd broken again.

They earned their food. The completion of chores or good behavior as befitting a Wheeler foster child would earn an extra spoonful for dinner. Neither the age nor the abilities of the child affected the chore allocation. Just yesterday, Ruby had to wash all the windows of the house, inside and outside. Little five-year-old Saira had to clean the oven. Ava at thirteen had mowed the lawn and weeded the garden, which she didn't mind doing since it kept her outdoors. But she didn't reveal this to Mrs. Wheeler who would reassign an enjoyed chore to a girl less willing. Ruby and Saira weren't strong enough to push the mower.

Which was why the three of them were always hungry, never completing their tasks within the time frame or to Mrs. Wheeler's satisfaction. Ava shivered, unfurling her fingers to pluck at her threadbare dress. The winter breeze sneaking under the back door along with the meager internal heating kept her cold. The only time she was warm was at night when they shared their cot.

Without a word, Ava rose to her feet, standing tall on trembling legs, struggling to keep herself upright while her vision spun. She turned to leave the kitchen.

Mrs. Wheeler's aged face mottled in anger, and spittle splattered her bottom lip. "And where do you think you're going?" Her shrill voice lodged Ava's heart in her throat.

"To the bedroom, mistress, to undress for my chastisement." She climbed the stairs, placing each foot with care. Through Mrs. Wheeler's bedroom, she trudged to the walk-in closet that was their shared room. With trembling fingers, she removed her dress, twitching as her skin chilled further. Willing her hands to settle, she shook them. A glance confirmed the weathered belt hung on a hook—its threat ever-present.

She felt no fear, had long ago given up on that emotion. It had served no purpose. Begging hadn't softened the monster's heart, crying either. Ava simply didn't respond anymore. Pain had no control over her, not since she'd discovered her happy place. It was returning to the real world she dreaded. She suffered from the pain then. Pulling her braid over her shoulder to trap it there, she dropped to her knees, bending over the cot. Resting the top half of her body on the thin mattress, she waited, her fists clenched and hidden under the cot.

Drawing in a deep breath, she let the warm sun call to her as it drenched the rolling green hills with the bright pink flowers that she didn't know the name of. She'd seen an image in one of Mrs. Wheeler's travel digi-zines. It had promised Ava a pain-free escape from the hell she lived in. She was enjoying running through the hills, stopping to pick flowers, and raising her face to the sunlight when Mrs. Wheeler's heavy tread neared. Ava refocused on the pink flowers. In her mind, a dark cloud formed on the horizon, marring the bright blue sky. That was when the first strike fell across her back.

Instead of the thundercloud alarming her, she turned away from it and bolted to an apple tree at the bottom of the meadow. Sometimes, the tree was an orange tree. Sometimes, when she needed it to be, it grew cupcakes, bright white ones with pink flowers and rainbow sprinkles. She remembered what those tasted like. A church lady had given each of the girls one, once. Heaven had coated her mouth with sweetness. The vanilla aroma was one she would never forget.

But she never knew what kind of tree she would find, and on awful days, when the clouds were stormy, the tree would change from apples to cupcakes. Like today. Tears flowed as she tried to reach the lowest branch, her fingers missing the enticing cupcake by a hair. With a whimper, she gave up, sitting against the trunk to watch the impending storm.

On the top of a hill, a policeman appeared. She froze. No one had visited her before. But this was her sanctuary. She could make his disappear. He waved a fist at the cloud, anger in his scrunched-up face. With a magical lasso, he captured the clouds and dragged them away. Sunlight burst upon her meadow, with more pink flowers blossoming. But the heat wasn't on her face or her black shiny shoes. It slashed across her back, burning until she dared not move.

A man with a uniform strode through her meadows, careful not to crush the blossoms. She'd seen his kind at the church fair when the pastor's wife had to be rushed to hospital. He had a kind face and drew closer to her hiding spot under the tree, a blanket in his hands. He flicked it open, offering to wrap it around her. It looked so warm that she nodded. But when it encircled her, the fire from her back burned through her body, and she cried out. She squirmed, trying to yank off the blanket.

Amid her wails, a cupcake fell from the tree into her lap. Her cries lodged in her throat, and when she looked down, the cupcake had turned into an apple. None of this had happened before, but the sight of it smothered the pain.

"Ava?" From afar, Ruby called to her. Ava jerked her head up to scan the horizon. "She's in her happy place, sir. She goes there when she's in pain or scared."

Ava frowned, wondering if Ruby was talking to the man with the red cross? Was Ruby in danger? Was she next? Ava snapped back to reality, the pain hitting her hard enough to suck the air out of her lungs.

"It's okay, angel. I have you," a gentle voice said.

She raised her eyes to look at the kind-faced man with a red cross on his shirt. "What...what happened?"

"Mrs. Wheeler forgot to lock the phone, so I called the police," Ruby said. "They came and took the monster away."

Chapter One

Earth
The Mirror Mirror Hair Salon
Year of 2252 April
Ten years later

Ava stared at her cold coffee. Her break was almost over, not that she cared. It was on days like today—overcast, the scent of rain in the air—the loss of her fiancé, Billy, brought her down hard. She drew in a shuddering breath, trying to not remember the fated night the policemen knocked on her door. Fred Munroe, her unofficial surrogate father, had peered over their shoulders, his face shadowed. His presence alone told her it was bad news.

Chills racked her body when she'd opened her front door to their dour faces, the rain pouring down around them, blue lightning striking in the distance. As dread squeezed like a tight fist around her heart, she ushered them inside. She recalled offering them coffee. Thankfully, they'd declined. Her hands had trembled. Performing the mundane task would have been beyond her. Fred had led her to the couch and sat beside her, his fingers gripping hers to lend her his strength. Despite her quivering bottom lip, she'd smiled, glad he was with her.

Gathering her courage, she'd uttered one word. "Billy?"

"I'm sorry, Angel." His voice was hoarse with emotion, and tears glistened in his dark green eyes.

"It happened quickly, Ava." Sheriff Sutherland wrung his hat in his hands. "He lost traction in the rain and collided with the big oak tree at Grayson Intersection."

Ava winced as she returned to reality, downing her cold coffee before washing her cup and leaving it on the drying rack. After the sheriff's statement, she'd lost all control—of her life, of her memories, of her heart. The weeks after were hell, and in a daze, she'd gotten through it. During that time, she'd lived more in her happy place than in the real world. Her surrogate sisters had supported her. Organizing the funeral, canceling the wedding arrangements, and ensuring she ate and slept a little. They didn't leave her alone, taking turns to stay with her. Even Fred had hung around. She'd cried more on his shoulder than anyone else's. Four years had passed. Time didn't heal all wounds.

"Why don't you go home early, Ava, sweetheart?" Her boss, Annie, wrapped an arm around her shoulders for a gentle squeeze. "You have no clients this afternoon, and I can see how the weather is affecting you."

"I have to get over him." Ava squared her shoulders. "Besides, what will I do at home? Cry?" Her heart constricted, and she shoved the familiar pain aside. Borderline desperate, she dialed Taylor, one of her adopted sisters. "Good afternoon, *Ms.* Montgomery. The Mirror Mirror Salon is running a promotion on blue hair dye..." Ava forced a chuckle and ignored Annie's deep sigh.

"Blue? What kind of a blue?" Taylor squealed.

"Lagoon blue. Ombre style with your platinum blonde locks would look stunning."

A shuffling, and other muffled noises almost drowned out Taylor's voice. "And will you shave the side like I've been begging you to?"

Ava slumped. "Yes." She slapped the mute icon just as Taylor screamed.

"I'm so there. I'm leaving now." A car door slammed.

Ava tapped the wall-mounted screen, ending the call, and grinned at Annie. "It seems I have a customer."

Her boss strolled away, shaking her head.

Ava shrugged and readied her station. Ten minutes later, Taylor burst through the salon's doors. The short, petite woman wore leggings, fuzzy bunny slippers, and a baggy T-shirt with oil paint on it in various stages of drying.

"You could've changed first," Ava teased. With Taylor, she'd fast learned to spread protective sheeting over the salon chairs.

"Are you insane? And have you change your mind?" Taylor rushed forward and came to an energetic halt next to Ava, bouncing on her toes. "Show me this *lagoon* blue."

Ava pursed her lips to hide her laughter and held out the sample.

Taylor stroked the faux hair. "It is a pretty blue."

"So, is that a yes?" Ava arched a brow.

"It's a hell yes." Taylor jumped up and down before sliding onto a plastic-covered chair in front of a wash basin.

Ava pumped up the chair, raising Taylor's shoulders to the porcelain basin's edge. "Got any news for me?" she asked as she wet Taylor's long platinum locks.

"I sold another two paintings."

"Oh, that's wonderful. Shall we celebrate this weekend?" Ava soaped Taylor's hair, massaging her scalp in the process before rinsing out the shampoo.

"Just as long as there are no romances. They depress me." Taylor offered an exaggerated pout.

"Deal." Ava added conditioner and massaged Taylor's scalp. "Where?"

"I think it's supposed to be at Vicky's house this time." Taylor's eyes widened, and she cupped her hand over her mouth. "But Melissa told me Jack had an accident about an hour ago."

Ava stiffened. She forced a smile. "Again?"

Jacqueline or Jack, another sister, was always getting hurt in some way. Courtesy of West Haven being a small town, they knew it the moment it happened. The town had two claims to fame, the Law Enforcement Training Academy where Jack worked and the Heavenly, Vicky's bakery.

"What happened this time?" Ava rinsed off the conditioner and patted Taylor's hair dry. With long strokes, she combed it, gentling her movements when she encountered snags.

"Bruised a few ribs."

Ava swallowed a sigh of relief. "Steve will try to use this, you know." She met Taylor's twinkling chocolate brown eyes.

"He can try. She won't budge on the height thing," Taylor tutted. "I mean, what is he, an inch shorter?"

"I don't know. For me, I don't find his baby curls attractive." What Ava wanted was a man, someone tallish, broad-shouldered, and not blond, like Steve or...Billy.

"Regardless, this town doesn't offer a lot in the way of men."

Ava frowned. "So, she should just settle?"

"Of course not. But she could get laid."

"Taylor?" Ava grinned while giving her a certain look. Taylor was as much a virgin as Jack was.

"I'm in love. Jack has no such excuse." Taylor followed Ava to the leather chair.

Ah, to be in love. She had loved Billy. The wedding arrangements had put a strain on their relationship, but she hadn't worried about it. Not until that fateful night. Only one reason explained why Billy was at the Grayson Intersection—Clarissa.

The woman had the nerve to show up at the funeral, and despite Jack, Taylor, and Vicky's anger, Ava hadn't minded. Clarissa had cried more than Ava had. Maybe she hadn't loved him enough? Maybe she could've been a better girlfriend, fiancé?

If he hadn't chased after that...nympho, he wouldn't have died. There was truth to that. Spinsterhood lay in her future. Maybe she should start gathering a few stray cats?

"Except I'm allergic," she muttered.

"To cats? You sure are. Remember that time you brought one home? It's the pinkest I've ever seen you." Taylor's sweet laughter served as the distraction Ava had needed.

As the storm raged outside, they giggled like silly schoolgirls. It was a pleasant way to while away the time. Taylor's hair came out lovelier than Ava had imagined. Even the shaving of her head on one side didn't irritate Ava as much as she thought it would. Taylor had a lovely shaped skull, with no scars, or dents. And the style suited her artistic friend. Even Annie stopped by to take photographs.

Taylor bounced with happiness. "Thank you for this, Ava. I feel so inspired. I'm rushing home to get my ideas down before they flitter away. Wanna come over later?"

"And watch you mumble as you smear paint on a canvas? No, but thanks." Ava smiled to soften her words as she folded the plastic sheeting. "I thought I'd drop by Heavenly to see what Vicky is up to."

"I bet you Antoine has her mumbling or screaming." Taylor laughed.

"He's like a child in a man's body." Ava grinned, picturing the pompous elderly French man who worked at Heavenly.

"Yip, always entertaining." Taylor kissed Ava on the cheek and squeezed her hand. "My door is open anytime, you know that, right?"

Ava flashed a genuine smile as she waved at Taylor through the shopfront.

"Now will you leave?" Annie folded her arms across her chest, Ava's bag and coat dangling from her fingers.

By the time Ava arrived at the bakery, the sun was hovering low in the sky, indecisive as to its destination. With a sigh, she yanked the door open and entered. The delicious aromas of cinnamon, apples, sweet confectionary, icing sugar, and chocolate greeted her. Vicky, all bounce and excitement, rushed toward her. Ava wondered if she would ever feel like that again. Climbing out of bed every morning had its challenges.

Vicky wore her chef's whites with a white double-breasted jacket that hugged her curves and houndstooth-patterned, blue and white leggings. She had tweaked the standard uniform for comfortability, and she was without the hat. Her rich, red-gold hair curled in a tight bun on top of her head, and her brown eyes sparkled.

"Hey, gorgeous, how was your day?" She wrapped her arms around Ava, surrounding her with a strong cinnamon aroma.

Drawing in a deep breath, Ava leaned back to grin at her friend. Taller than Vicky and Taylor who hovered at five-foot-four or five, she was nowhere near as tall as Jack. Ava was a mere five-foot-nine against Jack's six-foot-two.

Vicky ushered Ava to a table upon which sat a slice of her award-winning apple pie. With extra ice cream, just the way Ava liked it.

"You spoil me." Ava sat and tugged the plate closer. "I'm getting fat."

"Nonsense, you'll just jog further tonight." Vicky dropped into the opposite seat to watch Ava mumble and groan over each bite.

Ava was of medium build, not petite like Vicky and Taylor, not muscled like Jacqueline. Even though Ava was taller, she carried more weight on her frame. If she didn't run every day, she piled on the curves. There was also the sense of freedom she felt when she jogged like she didn't have a care in the world. Her current sanctuary. "I'm not running tonight. Playing cricket with the kids."

The idea of introducing the orphaned kids to cricket bubbled excitement from her belly to her chest. Once a week, she'd spend an evening at the local orphanage. They all did since they were orphans themselves. But Ava was far more dedicated. Vicky took cookies and sometimes baked with them. Jack taught them self-defense, which only upped the stakes among the boys. Taylor did painting lessons which most of the boys avoided since it was a girl thing to do. But nothing compared to the days when Michel 'Mich' Dunois visited them. Jack's astronaut older brother was handsome with his white-gold hair and sky-blue eyes. The boys hero-worshipped him. The girls all wanted to marry him. His visits were rare since he was off-world most of the time.

Vicky gasped. "Cricket? Are you sure?"

"Yes, it looked interesting. Last week we tried croquet. That *was* fun until Tommy whacked Mikey in the foot with the mallet." Ava laughed at Vicky's wide eyes. "It was a free-for-all after that. We have a new addition, as well. This time, a baby. The cities keep sending these abandoned children instead of arresting the birthing violations." Ava's breath shuddered out, a sense of helplessness numbing her arms.

"Heard about Jack?" Vicky waved a dismissive hand. "Of course, you have. Steve managed to get her to Fred's." She huffed, "He tried again."

"Knew he would, the idiot." Ava rubbed her stomach. "What's on the cards for you tonight?"

"I have a wedding cake to bake. Ms. Elise Barnard is finally marrying Ernest." Vicky flashed Ava a sassy grin. "The old woman wants a traditional fruit cake with marzipan. I tried to tell her, with a cake like that, I'd need more prep time, you know, to allow the brandy to soak in."

Ava paused, mid-wipe of her mouth with the paper napkin. "Oh no, how long have you had?"

"Four weeks. I added extra brandy to compensate, and hopefully, speed up the process." Vicky's eyes sparkled with mischief. "Each bite should suck the breath right out of her."

"Ernest will love it," Ava said.

They were the oldest dating couple in West Haven. He'd harangued Elise to marry him since her sixteenth birthday. She was seventy-two now and had agreed, at last. Now *that* was persistence. She'd once asked Ernest why he hadn't just found himself someone else. His response had stayed with Ava all these years.

"Dearest Ava, she infuriates me, yet I still want to be near her. It may be an obsession, but I always know when she is near with my heart melting when she smiles. If that's not something to fight for, then what is?" His eyes had misted with tears, and Ava's heart had swelled at the sight. What had hurt was that she hadn't felt this for Billy, not even a bit.

"Are we at Jack's tomorrow?" Vicky asked.

"I think so." Ava pushed her chair back and rose. "Thanks for the energy boost, Vicky."

"Sounds like you'll need it tonight." Vicky pulled Ava into a hug. "See you tomorrow."

Ava waved as she left, a smile on her lips. The best part was that she was still smiling by the time she reached the orphanage.

Chapter Two

KANZO STARED AT THE door before him as he waited for permission to enter. Shame and hope warred within him. Once it opened, he would take a step toward disobedience and dishonor. This action would cost him at least a foot of honor which, in Etterian terms, meant twelve inches of his hair. He caught his heel-length braid in his hand, stroking the tip as if this was farewell. But the ache in his chest drove him. A few days ago, they'd rescued a stranded Earthian...human. He recalled the day with clarity.

Tasked with the rescue, a unit had taken a kuta shuttle to the floating, white-suited male. They expected his life to have abandoned him, as his species had, but found him battling death. An image of his pale hair and ice-blue eyes came to mind. Despite his diminutive form, the human had honor. That was admirable and unexpected from a species whose planet was mid-grade at best. Michel Dunois was the human's name, and he'd one request, to bid his sister farewell.

But Kanzo's battle-bond and Supreme Commander Ulriq had denied the male this request and even though Ulriq had valid reasons, the decision didn't bring Kanzo peace. Alodon's balls, this was a *female* Michel wished to see. Honor demanded Etterians make the effort, no matter the obstacles. At Ulriq's announcement, Michel's disappointment contorted his body, his shoulders curled, and his mouth had drawn downwards. These humans were an expressive species.

"I'll speak to Sub-Commander Nerx. Perhaps he might urge Supreme Commander Ulriq to relent," Kanzo had vowed.

Only one of his battle-bonds had a sister, not that Kanzo had met her. Having a sister was rare and cherished in Etteria. Their females were birthing less and sparking fewer Etheras, the source of all matings. There were far too many males, and the statistics of finding one's Dar Eth mate leaned toward the impossible. Many of their males succumbed to the dark void growing inside them, losing their souls to loneliness. Such was their fate. For Ulriq to deny Michel such a blessed opportunity to bid a sister farewell was unforgivable.

Hope warmed Michel's face. "Is that possible? I understand there's a chain of command to follow, and I wouldn't want you to get into trouble on my behalf."

"I can ask." Kanzo activated his Optical Data Implant or O.D.I. embedded in his left wrist. Tapping on the holographic keys, he requested Nerx, Danic, and Aaro to attend him. They were Ulriq's closest battle-bonds, and if anyone could reach through to their stubborn supreme commander, it would be them.

"Summon me like I'm a *damu*?" Nerx strode in, unannounced.

The grumpy male glowered at Kanzo. A glance at Michel showed the human unintimidated. Danic dropped into a comfy as Aaro helped himself to the rehydrator.

"Michel, this is Sub-Commander Nerx, and Warriors Danic and Aaro. Nerx, you must speak with Ulriq." Kanzo hadn't wanted to waste a moment of Nerx's time. That worsened his demeanor, and for this to work, Kanzo needed him almost jovial. He smothered a snort, having set himself an impossible task.

"He denied the visit?" Nerx arched an eyebrow.

"I suspect he distrusts the Earthian, no offense." Aaro sipped his giyua juice. The tart fruit scented the air. "I would suggest eliminating what he might deem untrustworthy."

"Fit an O.D.I. with an activated tracker," Danic caught his braid and released it—a clear sign of agitation.

Kanzo forced himself to stand still. An unusual influx of energy pulsed through his veins, and he struggled to contain it. "Good, I'll have Medic Der attend to it. If this doesn't sway him?"

"Then we escort Michel ourselves." At Nerx's suggestion, the room fell silent and with valid reason. Etteria didn't tolerate disobedience. "We'll have to shuttle down. For an unknown planet, fauna and flora, and with our need for stealth, porting is unwise."

Less than a day later, Kanzo prepared to enter Michel's quarters to escort him to the waiting kuta shuttle. Danic would pilot. Afax had to be included in their disobedience to ensure their exit and return. Nerx had spoken to Ulriq and informed him of their plan, which concerned Kanzo. It wasn't logical to notify their commander they planned to disobey him.

As he escorted Michel through the docking bay, he tensed, scanning the hangar, expecting armed males to alter their course to security. His fingers brushed the grip of the blaster strapped to his thigh. Could he kill his males over this? He gritted his teeth. No, he'd stun only.

But no male rushed toward them, no battle cries pierced the silence, and no movement peeled out of the shadows. He ushered Michel to the hovering kuta shuttle nearest to the massive bay doors that towered the combined height of fifteen males. The propulsion was silent, the heat flowing around it bearable. Danic lowered the ramp. Stroking the cold Maloidian metal of the door frame, Kanzo entered.

"Don't you dress casually?" Michel dropped into a ketsi seat unaided. He didn't react to the adjusting chair as he had on his rescue flight. Kanzo smiled, wishing the human would cry out again and kick the chair. "You look like you're battle-ready."

While standing guard at the door, Kanzo glanced at Michel's soft blue pants and short-sleeved white tunic. All in his unit wore the same as Kanzo—black leggings in nano-polymer with multi-pockets and sleeveless armored vests, standard issue for Etterian males, including the heavy black boots.

"Etterians do not know *casual.*" Danic shook his head. He didn't turn to meet Michel's gaze while he tapped on the multi-lit console, preparing for flight.

"You do now." Michel flashed a smile but faltered when Ulriq stepped into the shuttle.

Kanzo jerked back, having not heard his battle-bond approach. Alodon's balls, he couldn't shoot him. Not Ulriq. Silence descended. The tension in the air thickened. Danic slid off the pilot's chair to face Ulriq. Aaro paused outside the kuta, waiting to board, but his shoulders were tense while he scanned the hangar, as Kanzo had done. Wincing, Kanzo stood to attention and waited for the command that would cost him his honor.

"You thought I would let you travel to the surface...*without* me?" Ulriq offered a stiff smile.

Kanzo released his breath, his shoulders relaxing.

"You're coming with?" Michel's bright smile contrasted with the heavy ambiance, as if the human couldn't sense danger. "You're going to love Jack, Supreme Commander."

Nerx bounded past a stiff Aaro and strode into the shuttle. Aaro followed, shutting the door behind him. Nerx nodded at Danic, a silent command to fly them planetside.

"I am pleased you decided to join us, Ulriq," Nerx said, though no expression crossed his features. "At least, I do not have to look at Michel's sour expression for a while."

Kanzo hid a smile, for there was no male more acerbic than Nerx. Michel bounced in his seat. His excitement scented the air like burned ozone.

Ulriq faced the human. "Tell me about your Jack."

"I have a fond memory from my childhood of her falling into a river. She climbed out of the water like a drowned rat, spluttering and cursing. That was when she gave me my first black eye for laughing at her, but it was worth it."

Rat? Black eye? Kanzo's O.D.I. flicked images and descriptions via his neural system, rushing to aid him. An unsavory description for one's sister. And good, she'd punched him in the eye.

"We spent the summer building that fort. Our neighbor was kind enough to supply the materials and tools." Michel gestured with his arms as if he rebuilt this *fort*.

The O.D.I.'s images indicated meter-thick walls, solid stone, and lookout points. Michel had built such a structure? What an odd thing to do as a *damu*. How large was it? Could it withstand an attack? Was it still standing? Kanzo opened his mouth to ask.

Michel swung his arm as if he hammered something. "We'd nailed it to branches extending over the river, thinking it a good strategy. It secured our fort, limiting its access to the one branch which wouldn't hold an adult's weight."

Kanzo snapped his mouth shut. Branches? As in a tree? Such a position could be defensible, but it couldn't have been built with stone. Unless Earth's trees were different from Etteria's? He snorted, visualizing the possibilities of such a structure precariously balanced on branches. But off the ground was good. Over a river granted it better protection against attacks from below.

"Little did we realize the branches might not hold our fort's weight." Michel chuckled, his bright eyes sparkling. "But it didn't collapse, no. The real reason Jack fell was due to a squirrel. It startled her, and squealing like a girl, she plummeted into the cold depths of the river." His shoulders shook as he laughed.

Kanzo struggled to follow the story. *Squirrel?* His O.D.I. revealed an adorable creature. Not that he distrusted this Jack's fear. Such a tiny creature could defeat a human when

Etteria's ocean omeika, no larger than his hand, could kill the hardiest of warriors. Except, the data the O.D.I. shared held no such reports of deaths by squirrel.

"To have her tell it, the squirrel was a snake as thick as my arm, and she lost her footing."

Kanzo pinched his brow, hoping to ward off the pulsing pain. *Snake?* Yes, a formidable creature for its speed, venom, and stealth. Squirrel versus snake? He too might have hidden the truth had a fluffy creature startled him.

"My Jack's hard on the outside but all sweet softness on the inside."

"We are all hard on the outside and soft on the inside," Aaro said, confusion furrowing his brow.

"Oh, no...it's a saying. It means you give the appearance of being impenetrable like nothing can hurt you. But on the inside, you are kind, understanding, compassionate."

"And your Jack is this?" Ulriq raised his hand to grip the safety loops as the shuttle tilted.

"Yes, you'll see." Michel grinned, energy vibrating off his smaller body.

Danic skirted the debris field orbiting the blue planet. The shields not only hid their presence but absorbed the damage should the abandoned pieces of metal strike them. A few did, but it was minor and ignored as he dropped through the atmosphere. It was a testimony to his skill that the ride was smooth, and the temperature within the shuttle remained cool despite the flames licking the shield.

Cobalt blue oceans greeted Kanzo, under skies the color of Michel's eyes. It was mesmerizing that such beauty existed despite the inhabitants polluting their water. Etterians valued their planet with pollution long eradicated. Their oceans were a vermillion from the schools of omeika infesting them. They'd done so for millennia, and it wasn't Etteria's way to exterminate them. Not to mention, those poisonous fish were a sought-after delicacy, their preparation requiring extensive training to bring out their unique flavor. Said flavor altered to the consumer's favorite foods as they ate. For planets such as Maloid, Sarvis, and Yithia, this was a miracle.

Bypassing domed villages as large as battleships, they darted over fields of gold, low enough for the shuttle's belly to brush the strange grass. Danic hovered the shuttle above an isolated structure before landing behind it.

"My house." Michel unbuckled, leaping to his feet.

Danic touched the kuta down with the barest of bumps while Kanzo's eyelashes fluttered as he absorbed images of houses or homes. A full-blown headache descended, pinging behind his eyes. They exited according to protocol, blasters drawn, gazes vigilant. Kanzo fell into place behind Ulriq. Years of excursions, battles, and infiltrations had taught him to follow without question. Fresh air greeted him. They halted outside the shuttle while Danic left it in stealth mode, marked the ground beneath the door, and drew his blaster.

They approached the dark-green door. Michel unlocked it with a swipe of his thumb and gestured them inside. They hurried past a food preparation room that overlooked a table with four metal chairs. These looked unyielding, unlike a ketsi seat with the ability to conform to an Etterian's shape. Open doors revealed sleeping quarters and a cleansing room.

With shoulders brushing the narrow confines of the passage, Kanzo passed an informal seating area before bursting outside into the pale-yellow light of Earth's one sun. When Ulriq nodded, they stowed their blasters and allowed themselves to relax. They took position at certain points and stood at ease, backs toward each other to scan the surrounding fields.

Kanzo tilted his face to bask in the warm sunlight. The sweet-scented air, expansive sky, sunlight, yes, he was pleased to be here. A tap on his arm snapped him out of his contentment. Michel handed him a glass bottle, condensation forming along its sides. Kanzo sniffed. Smoky bitterness, some plant matter, fermentation, and a hint of honey salivated his mouth. He sipped and moaned, the exotic flavors exploding across his tongue. Angling the bottle, he studied it. His O.D.I. translated the symbols. *Beer?* Another thing he liked about Earth.

The acrid stench of burning air drew his gaze. A gas fire flickered to life. Michel beamed, too pleased with himself. Kanzo smiled at his *damu*-like behavior. What a strange thing to waste one's time on.

Chapter Three

Earth

West Haven

The grand day of Mich's arrival

"Have you read this list?" Ava asked Vicky who sucked on a yet-to-be-paid-for lollipop. It was her second one, but the wrappers were in the cart. "Don't get me wrong. I'm excited to see Mich again, but this list... It's enough food to feed an army. Making your potato salad?" She held up a bulk bag of potatoes with one arm.

"Made it last night. My masterpiece requires prep-time."

"All your masterpieces require prep-time." Ava chuckled, then laughed when Taylor stumbled down the food aisle under a mountain of sodas.

"I'll get the garden salad ingredients, you help our vertically-challenged friend." Vicky rose onto her tiptoes to stretch across the tomatoes.

"Hey, I heard that." Taylor panted.

Ava snatched six packs out of Taylor's arms and stacked them in the cart. "Is that it?" She ran her finger down the tablet's screen.

"I hope so. Is there still time to help me find something to wear?" Taylor gestured to her cut-off jeans and a baggy T-shirt, both splattered with dried oil paint.

"What does it matter? It will have paint on it anyway," Ava teased.

"You're right. I should buy something...clean." Taylor's chagrin darted across her face. "A dress? Jeans? Can we browse now?"

"Of course we can. I'll just tell the butchery to hold the meat for us," Ava said.

Taylor pined for Mich, having always loved him. Ava studied her adopted sister and wondered how she managed to keep it together. The giddy feeling knowing that within an hour she'd be in the presence of her dream man? Ava missed that. Billy would steal a quick kiss, or he'd shower kisses along her neck. But more than that was coming home to a warm embrace after a long day.

"You know what? Stuff him. He wouldn't notice if I stood before him naked." The unexpected outburst startled Ava. She didn't know Taylor like this. "If he can't love me smelling of linseed oil with paint on my face then he can suck it."

Vicky gaped, her lollipop forgotten in her immobile fingers. "That's the best thing you've said in years."

"If there's nothing else, then let's go. Knowing Jack, even with her gunshot wound, she's parking her solarcycle in front of his house as we speak." Taylor grabbed a massive box of chocolates—the authentic kind—and dropped them into the cart. "Since Mich is paying, I'm getting these. We can share them later."

"Babe, I love this side of you." Ava resisted the urge to applaud and bounce on her heels as pride brought a tear to her eye.

"Good because it's here to stay."

"So, we'll drop by your house anyway?" Vicky said to which Taylor nodded, flashing a sheepish smile.

"Okay, but for a quick change. I can't believe Jack. Bruised ribs last week, a bullet wound this week, what's next?"

"A gorgeous man?" Ava forced a smile past the lump in her throat.

She hated it when Jack injured herself, and it happened too often. Losing someone was something Ava couldn't handle, not again. Vicky's answering snort and eye roll made Ava's smile genuine. She allowed the warmth of her sisters' company to hold back the hovering thunderclouds. With Mich here, her family was complete. Just for today.

"Gorgeous men? We'd have to go to the domed cities to find those." Vicky's skepticism was valid. Men were scarce in West Haven, and they had to find their heart palpitations somewhere else. "A rare species, I'm told." She pushed the cart through the automated scanner before running her wrist over the paypad. "Shit, I forgot Mich was paying. You owe me for those chocolates, Taylor."

"Fine, but then I'm not sharing."

"Fair enough." Vicky grinned and popped her lollipop into her mouth.

Engulfed by a wealth of love for her sisters, Ava smiled, content to observe their interactions. Within the hour, they were on their way to Mich's house near the outskirts of town. Taylor had thrown on the cleanest thing she had, and with a dab of lip gloss, was out the door. Ava had huffed when they made her sit in the back seat of Taylor's pink hybrid-coupe, but when she realized she could spread out her legs, taking up the entire back seat, she was happier. With the coupe's hood down, the wind tossed her hair. Sighing at her silly decision to leave it down, she gathered the ends and trapped them against her chest. Trust artistic Taylor to compare it to tar pouring over a shoulder.

But changing her hair color like she'd done Taylor's, was time-consuming. Black hair limited what dyes she could use. In the end, she let it grow out but kept the ends trimmed. Thank the Lord, she wasn't pale. Her toffee skin helped to give her color. Then again, her skin tone with her pale hazel eyes drew attention. She shrugged. Pretty eyes aside, she had a hell of a time shaving when black hair grew everywhere.

Taylor hit the dirt road without slowing down, tossing up dust in Ava's direction. She didn't have the heart to chastise Taylor who giggled like a child in a toy store. Ava brushed off her leggings and adjusted the wraparound blouse. Both were good choices—casual, comfortable, and a perfect outfit for a family gathering. Perhaps today, Mich, the idiot, might finally see what was before his eyes. He couldn't expect Taylor to wait forever for him.

As they pulled into the driveway, Ava tried not to gape at the group of men crowding the front lawn. Their military uniforms left nothing to the imagination. Black multi-pocketed pants into heavyset boots, weapons strapped to their thighs, sleeveless vests that molded to sculpted chests, and their heightened vigilance screamed military. Ava curled her fingers into fists, resisting the urge to fluff her hair. Five super-tall men—muscled and bronzed, proved that miracles still happened. Though how Earth Space Agency, Mich, and these men were connected remained a mystery.

CHAPTER FOUR

Earth

The Outskirts of a Human Village

Michel's Housing Structure

KANZO GLANCED AT THE chilled bottle in his long-fingered hand. The liquid was bitter and delicious. The alcohol tingled as it traveled through his veins. The sensation was brief though since his metabolism worked through the effects without allowing him time to fully enjoy it. He raised his gaze to the pale blue sky with the white fluffy clouds and winced at the brightness. The blue was strange. Etteria's skies were pink. But the warmth on his face was as pleasant, the cool breeze also so.

Ulriq might yet receive punishment for violating several ordinances regarding landing on Earth without permission and for rescuing an Earthian space traveler who hadn't requested assistance. Kanzo would offer to bear the punishment. So would several males under Ulriq's command. Well, they were the reason they were planetside in the first place.

They were experiencing a barbeque at Michel's housing unit. They gathered around a fire, for some strange reason, with the scent of it tickling Kanzo's nose. And when he'd enquired as to the reason they watched burning coals, Michel had responded, "It's what men do," as if that explained it. It didn't.

Cooking one's food source on an open fire was archaic by GC standards. Kanzo couldn't recall encountering a species that did this for...fun?

It *was* pleasant though, to sip his beer, and stare into the flickering flames.

"Who are we waiting for, Michel?" Aaro asked.

"My sisters." The male shrugged, lifting the beer to his mouth, even as a smile formed.

"You have more sisters?" Danic arched a brow. For an Etterian male to have a single sister was a true blessing, but to have many...

"I thought you only had Jacqueline?" Kanzo asked, proud of himself for remembering her unusual name.

"Jack is biologically my sister, the other three I adopted."

Yet another reason to admire the human. To assume protection of defenseless females was honorable. Kanzo stared at the pale-haired male, at how such a small being could be this honorable.

His coloring was also startling. Kanzo was used to Etterian males—all similar in height, bronze skin tones with fish-tail-braided black hair falling to their heels and equally well-muscled from extensive weapons training.

From a young age, Etterians learned unarmed combat known as Hatimaye to assist in controlling their emotions. Tolerated emotions were humor or righteous anger. Only with a female may they show affection and lust, to a certain degree. But then again, the females were as unemotional as the males.

Their lack of emotions meant their eyes remained a constant dark blue. Sometimes, depending on how traumatic the incident, the male's eyes might flicker to ice-blue. This was why he'd thought Michel was an Eth—a male who'd experienced the Ethera and had a mate, a Dar Eth.

But finding one's life mate was rare. So, Etterians based alliances on mutual need or political aspirations. Kanzo had no remarkable lineage. No Etterian females sought him out for reproduction. Even Nerx, a sour-tempered male, was an interest to their females.

A deep rumble penetrated his thoughts. Kanzo glanced in that direction. In the distance, a being straddled a two-wheeled mechanical contraption, disturbing the sand on the road. The machine maneuvered well, despite the shifting sand beneath its wheels.

The being wore all black like Etterian warriors. He grasped his blaster as his bonds did. The helmet the being wore looked similar to Michel's when they'd rescued him. Was this being a threat or a possible space traveler, as well? The machine pulled up in front of them, dust and mechanical oil scents engulfing them in a cloud. It irritated his eyes, but he didn't look away, his muscles tense and ready. A strange sweet scent permeated the dust, bringing one thought to his mind. Female.

Underlying her fragrance was the salty tang of blood, as if she sported an injury. Relaxing, he shifted closer to admire the machine. It was some sort of transport device?

The black metal was appealing, the sound it made, thrilling. It had droned and rumbled, but now, it tinkled as if heated metal cooled.

They circled the female as she swung a leg over the back of the machine and pulled off her gloves. The black fabric hugged her figure like a second skin. It didn't look as if she carried any weapons. The gloves hid tiny hands with short fingernails. He watched with bated breath as she unclipped her helmet and yanked it off to reveal flowing waves of sun-white locks. The color matched Michel's hair.

This was Jacqueline? Human females were beautiful. He gritted his teeth, fighting the unexpected and unwanted swell of excitement.

He assessed her figure again. Yes, beautiful. She spun to bury her gloves in her helmet before slipping it over the front of the machine. Michel burst out of the housing structure. Gripping his blaster, Kanzo faced him. Michel tossed the beers at Danic before he yanked the female into his arms.

"Jack." He crushed her against him in a public show of affection.

"Holy shit, dammit. Put. Me. Down." Her cry of pain had Michel dropping her. He held her away from his body to study the length of her. "Bloody time you came home." The smile that spread across her face was exquisite, full of emotions Kanzo couldn't identify.

"What happened this time?" Michel gestured to her body.

"I'll fill you in later. Tell me, why is there a stripper convention happening here?" She met Kanzo's gaze, fearless in her perusal, before facing Michel. "And in bronze glitter?"

Glitter? The O.D.I. rushed to inform him, and with a scowl at the description, Kanzo glanced at his battle-bonds only to see them doing the same.

"We don't sparkle," Nerx growled, too low for humans to hear.

"Shit, I almost forgot. Come meet the Commander." At Michel's words, Nerx and Danic parted to allow them through.

Kanzo returned to the fire and sipped his beer, content to watch Michel introduce his sister to Ulriq. The white-gold of her hair cascaded around her in wild abandonment. Perhaps it was the freedom of it that Kanzo appreciated. He glanced at his battle-bonds and grinned at their fascination.

"Ulriq, this is my sister, Jacqueline."

Danic lunged as Ulriq paled, shuddered, and threw out his hand to lean against the housing structure. Nerx stopped Danic with a firm grip on his shoulder, his gaze telling them to wait. Before them, Ulriq's eyes changed to ice-blue as the famed Ethera struck him down. His great body trembled, a fine sheen of sweat coated his skin, and his muted grumble made Kanzo wince.

He gaped at Jack, his senses numbed. The Ethera was rare. He couldn't recall when the last pairing had occurred. And that his supreme commander was the male to receive such a blessing made their disobedience worth it. Perhaps King Xeus would be more lenient, considering that Ulriq hadn't wanted to come planetside in the first place.

Kanzo pinched his lips, reaffirming that he didn't long for such a gift. It was futile to waste one's hopes and dreams on an impossible occurrence. And perhaps Jack was an oddity on her world? Surely no more Dar Eths could be found on this mid-grade planet.

"Alodon's balls, Kanzo. Did you see?" Danic bounced on his toes.

Kanzo nodded but didn't look up to meet his gaze. He would see hope there. How could he reveal his deepest fear, that Danic's excitement would trigger an answering longing? He focused on his hearing and dimmed it so he wouldn't have to listen to the conversation around him, anything not to hear their joy. Ulriq finding his Dar Eth didn't mean they would find theirs.

He far preferred to live his life as per Base Commander Remi's example, to face the void on a battlefield. Danic tapped his shoulder to get his attention. Kanzo increased his volume to address him, hoping the male had remembered that to feel was to fail—their Etterian mantra.

"The sisters are arriving." Danic gestured to the pink ground vehicle traveling down the road.

One of the three females had black hair—Kanzo nodded. A female should have black hair, like his. Jack and Michel's hair color was too striking for his liking.

The vehicle stopped, and three females climbed out, surrounding him with a cloud of scents—sweet, spicy, delicious. He drew in a deep breath, unable to stop himself.

"What the hell, Jack? Are these men edible?" The black-haired female circled the ground vehicle to wrap her arms around Jacqueline with the utmost care.

Kanzo studied her, admiring her long and toned legs in skin-tight pants, with a flowing tunic belted around her waist. The garment was semi-transparent, displaying the curves of her lovely breasts. His malehood stirred, and he scowled. It shouldn't move without stimulation. Her voice was husky and sensual, he liked how it caressed his skin, and her scent was sweet, enticing. He drew in another breath.

"They can hear you, babe," Jacqueline teased her.

"What? Men who listen? Have we died?" The red-haired female laughed. Her garments hugged a figure sensual, feminine, and curvier than any female he'd ever seen.

"Damn, and I thought Mich was tall." The last female circled the vehicle in a long skirt. She was tiny. Her white-blue hair fell around her in waves, brushing a shoulder. Her scent was strange—chemical and sharp.

"Is that my girls I hear?" Michel welcomed each one, dropping a kiss on their cheeks. "I promised to explain what quantum mechanics is..." He grinned at their longsuffering groans. "Okay, don't kill me, let me introduce you."

Danic nudged Kanzo as they watched Michel escort the females to Ulriq. "I did not know that females came in such variety."

Kanzo's gaze traveled over them with his gaze returning to rest on the black-haired female no matter how many times he glanced away.

"And this is Danic, Aaro, Kanzo, and Nerx." Michel's voice dragged Kanzo's gaze from his beer, forcing him to analyze how his heartbeat fluttered. His throat constricted, and the blood rushing through his veins was akin to pre-battle excitement.

"It's a pleasure to meet you." The blue-haired female offered her hand. "Such unusual names, whereabouts are you from?"

"Europe," Jacqueline blurted. "They're from northern Europe."

Kanzo's gaze riveted on the black-haired female as she smiled at him. She was mesmerizing. His heart ceased beating as he admired the curve of her neck, brushing over her pointed chin to rest upon her mouth—they appeared soft. He forced himself to look away, to travel along her tilted nose to meet her exquisite pale-green eyes.

Heat so painful it bordered on pleasurable lanced through him, snatching his breath, gripping his mind, holding it hostage, and forcing him to the green terrain. He dropped to a knee, his hand slamming down on the ground to stop a full descent. Unbearable fire coursed through his veins with a direct path to his malehood. Groaning in agony, he hardened to an incredible length, his body shivering. Tingles rippled through him from his nape to his toes, and he moaned in pleasure. An image of her burned into his vision. Her bare long legs entwined with his, his hips nestled between hers, his shaft pressed at her channel, her entrance wet, hot, and so soft. A musky, addictive scent lingered, that of her arousal.

In the vision, he opened his eyes to watch her head fall back as her kiss-swollen lips parted on a husky cry. It originated from the back of her throat. A gasp drew him back to reality, and he wished it hadn't since she'd rushed forward to help him. He shuddered, her feather-light touch on his shoulder hardened his nipples, and his stiff malehood twitched in anticipation. Then the scent of her arousal reached him, and what control he'd fought for splintered.

"You smell...good," he said, his voice above a whisper, his tone almost accusing.

Her scent had altered, revealing her aroused state. Did it have to be so enticing, and as enthralling as he envisioned?

"Is that a bad thing?" Her breathtaking eyes widened.

"Yes, for now, it is." He ran his gaze over her exposed collarbone, and this close, her pebbled nipples. His eyes burned with the same pain as his loins, but he wouldn't glance away.

"You are fine?" She pursed her full lips.

He fought the urge to tease them apart with his own. To taste her—he was certain she was sweet. He wanted to hear her breath hitch, to hear her whimper and cry out as she'd done in his vision.

"I am." His rough voice contradicted his words.

She rose and left him without another word. A harsh emotion cinched his chest in a vise. He had done or said something now that had cost him more than he could fathom.

Chapter Five

"WHAT THE HELL JUST happened, Ava?" Vicky asked as she unpacked the groceries.

Ava couldn't bear to watch the calm methodical movements. She paced, clenching and relaxing her fists. Fury pummeled her, driving her to punch something. When she'd climbed out of the car to face a wall of sheer masculinity, the back of her neck had tingled. She'd barely resisted fluffing her dust-layered hair.

One man had snagged her attention, skittering excitement along her senses as if she was a teenager again.

When he'd dropped to his knee like the Camelot knights of old, she'd frozen, too in shock to react. He'd raised his sky-blue gaze to her, intensity swirling in their magnificent depths.

His wide cheekbones were the same width as his square jaw. Surprising her was this need to run kisses along his jawline's rugged edges. The man's nose was long with a dimple on the tip, and his wide flat upper lip over a fuller bottom lip made it appear as if he pouted. It was sensual, that bottom lip. And his ice-blue downturned eyes under arched, coal-black eyebrows were mesmerizing against his bronzed skin.

His body made her drool. No man had a right to be so tall, so broad-shouldered, so muscled. He could pick her up without breaking a sweat. His uniform hugged him like a second skin, and it made her realize, as her gaze had traveled down his muscled torso, narrow waist, and hips, that she was a thigh girl. Damn, did he have sexy thighs. His were thick and strong, which his black military pants did nothing to hide.

She clenched hers together as her desire drenched her panties for the second time since meeting him. The other men were as tall, as dark-haired, as muscled, but there was just something about him that called to her. He'd glanced at her, and she'd almost swooned at his feet. Those ice-blue eyes held an emotion her heart understood.

"I don't know. The idiot fell to a knee then complained about how I smelled." She sucked in sharp breaths, trying to calm the inner turmoil churning her gut. If she prodded the volatile lump, it wasn't just fury but disappointment. She slumped and shivered, rubbing her arms from elbows to shoulders.

"They are foreigners, maybe you should give him a break." Vicky reached for the cutting board. "Can you clean the lettuce for me?"

Ava flashed an apologetic smile, took a deep breath then crossed to the sink. "You are right. I'm overreacting." She pulled apart the lettuce with too much force, then held the leaves under the water, and allowed the cool water to soothe her.

"They're gorgeous, though. Did you see their hair?" Vicky's attempt at a distraction worked.

Ava smiled, imagining running a hand down his thick braid. "It shines. They must take good care of it."

"It's just strange that they all have these long braids."

"Foreigners remember?" Ava rinsed the lettuce again before dumping the shredded leaves into a bowl. "I liked the look of him, Vicky. I haven't felt like that in ages, not even with…" She bit her lip before she mentioned Billy.

"That should give you hope." Vicky looped her arms around Ava's waist, giving her a hug from behind.

"What's happening?" Taylor strode into the kitchen, her skirt sashaying around her. "What can I do to help?"

"Huh?" Ava frowned and pulled out of Vicky's death grip. "You usually hover at Mich's elbow."

Taylor flicked a dismissive hand. "Like I said, he can suck it."

"Love that, babe, but we know how you feel. Spend the time with him while he's here," Vicky tossed over her shoulder as she rinsed carrots.

"I'm tired of hovering. If he wants to see me, he can come find me." Taylor climbed onto a barstool, a common occurrence due to her short stature. "So, what happened to Kanzo, Ava?"

"Kanzo?" Ava stilled, rolling his name across her tongue.

"I don't know. He fell to a knee. Weirdest thing I've ever seen," Vicky said as she sliced the tomatoes as only a chef could. "It looked knightly."

"It looked painful." Taylor stole a carrot to nibble on, dodging Vicky's slaps.

"I offered to help, but he was too macho to accept help from a mere woman," Ava said breaking apart the feta. She caught Taylor throwing a concerned look at Vicky and abandoned the feta before only crumbs remained.

"On another note, I tried something stupid yesterday." Taylor sucked on her fingertips after having stolen slivers of tomato. "In honor of the years wasted pining for Mich, I waxed...y'know...down there."

Ava gasped and swallowed a giggle. "You did what?"

Pink splashed across Taylor's cheeks. "You know me, I don't do anything by half measures. I was careful, and it went well. Just figured, since I had wax left over, that I might as well do my legs too."

"Oh, boy." Vicky's shoulders shook as she tossed a salad with tongs.

"Maybe I was too confident. So close to finishing my thighs, I entangled the wax strips and removed half the hair from my forearm and any backside fluff on my right cheek."

Laughter gurgled up from Ava's belly, unable to hold it back any longer. It felt so good to laugh, and as she wiped away the tears, she strained to hear what Taylor said next.

"I had to wax my butt and forearms, as well," she said with a self-deprecating chuckle. "I now have an ass as smooth as a baby's."

Just imagining Taylor's screams and curses, tears blurred Ava's vision. She giggled to herself while spreading out the salads on the table alongside the barbecue. As soon as her hands were free, she tugged Taylor into a crushing hug, almost squashing the bread rolls she carried, and pressed a kiss to her temple.

"Please fetch the sauces for me, Ava?" Vicky asked as she arranged the table, leaving space for the meat Michel was preparing. "And the cutlery if you don't mind."

Ava released a shuddering breath and ran into the house. She ducked her head, her senses prickling as if all eyes were on her, including her knight's. She shivered. That giddy feeling she'd envied Taylor for settled in her chest. And for a moment, Ava relished it.

"You are staring."

Kanzo granted Danic a glance, acknowledging the truth in his statement. His gaze returned to admiring the human female he'd just met. Her laughter moved through him, striking him hard. His breathing labored as he watched her shoulders shake, her breasts bounce—the joy erupting from her was intoxicating.

"What can you expect, Danic?" He frowned at this new development, this attraction. Despite his efforts otherwise, he was joyous with a smile twitching his lips. The fiery burn of fury wrestled with the sweetness of happiness like he'd lost control of himself. Etterian males strived for stoicism, so to experience intense happiness and pleasure was something Kanzo didn't know how to deal with. "She is my Dar Eth." Speaking it aloud solidified his new reality. As if he received a punch to the head, he sat there, stunned, in horror, in disbelief, and with a throbbing yearning that surprised him.

"You did not want one, I know."

Kanzo's gaze feathered across the unclaimed human females, Vicky and Taylor. His focus darted to the tall female, Jacqueline, who'd called forth his Supreme Commander Ulriq's Ethera. Then shifted to the black-haired, green-eyed female who had started his own. All in one day. These females were precious gifts, and if more females could spark Etheras for Etterian males, perhaps there was one for Danic on Earth too. Kanzo released a deep sigh. This gift was from the Maker, yet he'd never believed, never longed for a female to call his own. Danic would sacrifice so much more for such a privilege.

"To live just for her? How can a male hand over his strength, his very breath to a female? It is insane."

"A Dar Eth will not demand such a sacrifice," Danic said with absolute conviction.

A *damu*'s response to his predicament. Kanzo snorted. "It does not matter. I do not know her."

"True, but she is not Etterian. You cannot treat Ava as you would one of ours."

"Do not say her name," Kanzo growled, startled at the dart of angry heat scorching his chest.

Danic tilted his head, his gaze calculating. "As a human, she will not feel the same effects as Etterians. If you do not want her..."

The implication that Danic could steal his Dar Eth angered Kanzo further, and he thumped his friend on the arm hard enough to bruise. Just let him try to take her. But Danic's calculating expression remained. Kanzo didn't like seeing it, not one bit.

Chapter Six

Kanzo accepted the offered plate from Vicky who flashed him a look he didn't understand. He thanked her and stared at the meal before him. His Dar Eth's name was Ava—short, sweet, and perfect. But hearing it from Danic had irritated him. He scowled at his plate, hating feeling the anger, the irritation, the longing. Hating feeling any emotion. To feel is to fail. And he was failing.

"I'm surprised you don't have food like this in your country. This is steak, a hot dog, potato salad, and a green salad. They're delicious." Ava's voice so near startled him. How had she managed to sneak up on him? He should've at least scented her approach.

"Which is your favorite, Ava?" Danic drew her attention away from Kanzo.

He scowled again.

"The potato salad." She hummed. "Vicky makes the best salad. I had it on Sunday, but I could eat it every day."

Under her vigilant gaze, Kanzo scooped a dollop into his mouth. He rumbled his approval at the salt-tangy flavor coating his tongue.

"Would you like another beer? A soda?" she asked.

"What do you prefer?" At Danic's innocent question, she chuckled, the sound rasping along Kanzo's taut nerves.

"I hate beer, sorry." She shrugged.

Kanzo admired the way her eyes crinkled at the corners as if she was often joyful. "Then a soda please," he said before Danic could.

She faced him, her gaze wary. "Which one?"

"Your favorite," Danic said, receiving another scowl from Kanzo.

Ava laughed and sashayed away.

Kanzo watched her backside sway as she disappeared inside the housing structure. His mouth dried, and he struggled to swallow his mouthful of food past the lump in his throat. Watching her return was even better, the bounce to her breasts, the indent of her waist, the swing of her hips, the smile on her lips, and the sparkle in her green eyes did nothing to calm the fire barreling through his body.

"I brought you the most popular. Mine is cherry flavored, but not many people like that." She gave them each a red can, popping the lid for them before offering Nerx and Aaro the same.

In Michel's Kitchen

"Have you eaten something, Ava?" Kanzo's friend asked a while later, as he brought his plate into the cooking area.

She snapped her gaze from the window. The wind rippled across the wheat fields, shimmering like liquid gold. "You have me at a disadvantage. I haven't learned your name."

"Warrior Danic et Ynic." He pressed his fist to his chest in a salute, his shoulders stiffening. "You implied you enjoy this potato salad, but you did not eat."

"I'm not hungry, not today." She forced a tight smile. "They've all forgotten, and that's a good thing. Just wish I could forget." She shook herself before she faced him. A lump lodged in her chest, like an encroaching blackness, stopping her from spewing her sorrow and anger. What was it about strangers that made it easier to spill one's secrets and true emotions? "Do you need anything? Another soda?"

"What is special about this day?" Danic placed his plate down then balanced one hip on the edge of the counter.

She studied his posture and the determined look he leveled on her. "I lost my fiancé four years ago today." To hide her trembling fingers, she latched onto a small towel which she unfolded and refolded.

Danic gasped, slicing a glance down the passage to the door leading to Kanzo. Now that was revealing. "You had a mate?"

Mate? As in soul mate or did he mean partner? She followed his gaze, half expecting Kanzo to show himself. "No, almost a mate. He died a few weeks before we..." Her breath hitched, and she threw down the towel. "I thought I was over it, but this was the day I found out Billy didn't love me, that he much preferred Clarissa's arms to mine."

"He had another female? That is dishonorable," he growled, revealing a little fury even when his face remained stoic.

At the anger in his voice, Ava stilled. "I don't know why I'm telling you this, Danic. I'm sorry."

"I am pleased to listen to any words you speak, Ava," he said, his tone formal.

A rat-a-tat came from the front of the house. She bolted from the kitchen just as Kanzo ran toward her. His eyes were narrowed beneath his furrowed brow.

"Yithians," he yelled at Danic, before swinging Ava up and over his shoulder.

Her squeal was cut off when her stomach hit his shoulder, and his hand rested on her backside. Not that he cared as he sprinted through the house to the backyard. She lifted her head to look behind them. Aaro had Vicky over his shoulder, Taylor over Michel's. Nerx supported an injured Ulriq while Jack and Danic fired strange-looking weapons at the...spaceship in the sky.

Ava gaped at it. She knew there were aliens, but she doubted she'd see any in her lifetime. Her glance flew to the side as realization dawned. Kanzo and Danic were aliens? Holy cow, how could she not have seen the obvious? Their skin was bronze. But she had believed Jack, had thought they stemmed from somewhere on Earth where that skin tone was prevalent. Blood rushed to her head due to her position. It would hide the flush of humiliation flushing her face.

They boarded a spaceship, and Kanzo lowered her into a seat, his touch gentle. He strapped her in before assuming the seat next to her. His breathing labored but not from having run carrying her weight since he hadn't broken a sweat. No, from having to touch her. He shifted away from her if she leaned closer to him like he hated her near him.

His distaste was like a slap to her face. Gripping the chair, she squeezed her eyes shut against the pain lashing her chest. She held her breath until her lungs screamed with fire forcing her to suck in air. Glancing down was the only way she could hide the tear that escaped. Maybe if she kept her eyes shut no one would notice? If she didn't brush the tear away no one would comment? And worse than the fear that someone would notice, was the fact that no one did.

Jack entered the craft, making demands. Danic's responses were calm. The craft lifted off the ground, slamming Ava's heart into her stomach. It didn't matter, nothing mattered past the sharp pain crippling her. Why had Kanzo bothered to rescue her if he hated her so much? Why had he taken the seat next to her? Danic, who'd been sweet and kind to her, could've rescued her. She didn't speak, didn't move, just forced herself to breathe in and out, waiting for the dark spots in her vision to dissipate. Crossing her arms over her chest, she scowled instead, rejoicing in the self-directed anger beginning to uncoil in her.

What kind of idiot would she be to endure Kanzo's disgust? Why didn't he just leave her alone, why force himself to save her, to sit next to her? She wasn't an idiot. Never again would she sit by and let a man hurt her. That Ava had died with Billy.

Strange tingles began at her extremities before sweeping through her body. Startled, she raised her hand to stare at her fingers as they faded.

"Kanzo," she screamed, her voice filled with fear despite her determination not to ask him for help.

He spun to look at her, and his beautiful eyes widened. At that moment, time slowed. Fear, disbelief, pain, and panic darkened his handsome face just before he lunged for her.

On the kuta shuttle.

Kanzo stared at her empty seat, riveted by shock before he unstrapped and bounded up, roaring from the unbearable pain lancing through him. It tightened his chest like someone had reached through him and squeezed every drop of blood from his heart.

"What now?" Nerx said as he tended to Ulriq's wound.

"Ava," Kanzo roared, not caring that screaming her name didn't help matters. "Ava!" The pain inside demanded he react. Trapped in a shuttle with no idea where she was or who had taken her, struck him with such helplessness, almost paralyzing him.

"Where is Ava?" Aaro gripped Kanzo's shoulder, the concern rising in his voice calmed Kanzo a little. His battle-bond would understand.

"She was ported," Kanzo whispered, his hands switching between clenching and rubbing his face. "We must go back."

"We cannot. Ulriq needs urgent assistance," Nerx said.

Kanzo's vision darkened, and the void rose to engulf him. He clasped his head with his hands. "She's my—"

"I know exactly what she is, Warrior Kanzo. Who took her? Where is she now?" Nerx remained focused on Ulriq's back, even though he directed his questions to him.

"Comm Prex and Ksal, have them investigate immediately." Ulriq narrowed his ice-blue gaze, his understanding clear.

"Doing that now," Danic called from the pilot's seat.

"Ava needs you to focus and remain calm. We are her only hope." Aaro's words reached through to Kanzo. He grabbed him by his upper arms, forcing Kanzo to meet his gaze.

"You did not see her fear, Aaro." Kanzo relived her reaching for him, silently pleading with him to save her. "She was scared. I am supposed to protect her. And I—"

"Alodon's balls," Aaro growled.

Kanzo's vision went black.

Chapter Seven

A Cold Metallic Cell

AVA BLINKED AT WHAT looked like the inside of another spaceship. This one smelled funny, like decaying organic matter, and it was too cold. She shivered while studying her surroundings from the position of a hard-grated floor—the same gray metallic walls as in Kanzo's spaceship. But where theirs had comfortable seats, this one had nothing. As she shifted, nausea hit her, and she doubled over, moaning, swallowing the urge to throw up. Half-digested potato salad pooled on her tongue. A hissing penetrated her shocked mind, growing louder as it neared.

The moment the two creatures stepped through a hidden door, she knew she was in serious trouble. They looked like humanoid sharks. Their skin was gray and shiny. She stiffened as they approached. Their solid black eyes showed no expression. She wasn't even certain they were looking at her. There were no pupils she could discern. One creature hissed something to the other, and she gasped, seeing tiger teeth peeking through his wide lips. His gesturing was violent with his three-fingered hands, then he slapped the other alien across the face.

He pointed at her, the hissing continuing at a frantic pace. The hissing must be their language. The subordinate alien lunged toward her, and she squeaked, clambering away from him. Her situation settled on her with a deafening roar.

She was so screwed.

The alien grabbed her, his clammy hand cupping the side of her head. No matter how she struggled, she couldn't shake him off. He spat-lisped words, then slammed her face down, pinning her to the grated floor. When she squirmed, he rested his chest on her shoulder, holding her still. Fire enflamed her ear. She screamed as agonizing shards of glass pierced her skull, tearing her eyes. When he rested his weight on her hip to stand up, she groaned. She lay on the floor, grateful for the cool metal against her throbbing cheek. She didn't care, the excruciating pain in her ear was her only focus. The alien hissed again, and this time his words speared her skull. She whimpered.

"Curse your gods, you are the incorrect female ported. My incompetent soldier took the female closest to the wounded Etterian."

She gaped, blinking at him. He spoke English? Wincing at each word he spoke, she tried to understand him. Did he mean Ulriq?

"Who were you after?" She pushed herself into a sitting position. And for her trouble, received a three-fingered slap. Her head whipped to the side. She cried out, catching herself from hitting the floor. With a moan, she choked on the thick salty blood while her tongue tested the cut on her bottom lip.

"You will never speak to me, Etterian scum."

She frowned. He thought her Etterian? Perhaps it was her black hair? It was the only common denominator. She opened her mouth to correct him, but at the metallic tang of her blood, she pinched her mouth shut. Let the idiot think whatever he wanted to. Earth wouldn't launch a rescue, but the Etterians might, especially if Mich and Jack demanded it. She couldn't allow herself to lose hope.

"We will have to use the device," the leader growled, his ferocious scowl painting his features in an evil light—the slanted and narrowed eyes in solid black, the wide mouth pinched into a thin line, and his hand resting on a weapon of some sort strapped to his belt.

"As you command, Operative Twyl," the soldier lisped.

The leader…Twyl left Ava alone with her abuser.

She studied him, wondering if he would release her now.

"You have cost me much, female." The alien's resentment dripped from his lips.

She wanted to smack him, and if she had the energy, she might have attempted it. She'd costed him? What had his stupidity cost her?

"May I speak?" she hissed and gaped. Her words weren't in English.

The alien raised his hand, and she flinched, then held herself still, expecting a slap any second. When nothing happened, she cracked an eye open to meet his gaze. His facial expression was calculating. She didn't like it.

"Speak," he commanded her as if he had the right.

As her jailer, he did.

"Who were you after?" Twyl had said she was the wrong female. Which meant Taylor, Vicky, or Jack? Her mouth dropped open as cold settled in her bones. They wanted Jack. She had fired at the spaceship. Was this a revenge kidnapping? "White hair? Taller than me?" she asked to confirm her suspicions.

His smile spread into a wide grin, revealing two wicked teeth protruding over his bottom lip. Her skin crawled. What were these creatures? Humanoid sharks with sabretooth canines and evil?

She nibbled on her lip then yelped as the sting of her cut made its presence known. What were they going to do with her? Why did they want Jack? But Ava held back. She wasn't going to give them information they could use.

A rescue had to come. Mich would insist. Jack might throw a tantrum. But would the Etterians assist? Her thoughts flashed to Kanzo's last expressions. Fear had widened his eyes before he'd cared enough to lunge for her. She didn't place any hope in his reaction. A hated enemy might try to help a falling opponent. His actions didn't mean he cared for *her*. She fluttered her eyelashes, stemming the tears stinging her eyes.

The slap across her bruised ear bounced her face off the grated floor. Her cheekbone stung. She cried out but didn't get up. What was the point? The alien ass would just strike her again.

"I spoke to you, slave," he spat.

She settled her gaze on him, moaning at the sharp pain in her ear. His lisped words hurt like hell, vibrating the wound and spiking fresh agony through her skull. She didn't break eye contact, not willing to show him subservience. If he wanted to kill her, then he'd better get on with it. She waited for him to repeat whatever he'd said to her. When he didn't, she chanced sitting up.

"Hit her again, and you will die, Hlar." Twyl's words reverberated through the cell, piercing her skull anew.

She whimpered, pressing her hand to her ears to block his hissing. Something warm and wet coated her skin. She glanced at her blood-stained palm and raised a glare at the alien...Hlar.

"Are you insane?" she gasped. "What the hell did you put in my ear? Whatever it was, it was poorly done." She jumped to her feet, showing him her bloody hand as evidence.

"You remove it, now!" Panic drove her voice higher. Fear of the unknown object now in her head seized her breath in her chest.

A tracking device? A translator? A bomb? An insect? She shivered at the last one. Hlar lunged for her, swinging his hand as if to slap her again. This one she dodged, but his other hand she didn't see coming until the last moment, but she wasn't fast enough.

Pain and stars burst across her vision. As she hit the floor, disorientated, the door opened. Twyl strode through and fired his strange weapon. Hlar's lifeless body landed beside her. She blinked at his soulless eyes staring at her. The horror didn't have time to settle within her. Twyl's black boots near her nose drew her dazed notice.

"Stupid Etterian," he hissed, turning his gun on her.

A thousand wasps stung her body, spasming each muscle. The sharp bites were too much for her brain to process. Numbness set in while she twitched on the floor.

That was sort of painless was her final thought as death claimed her.

Chapter Eight

Etterian Battleship, Kushin
En route To Mascroba, Yithia
Medical

"If you go berserk again, I will put you under for longer," Medic Der said to Kanzo as soon as his eyelids fluttered open.

"Ava," Kanzo moaned. Something squeezed his chest, so tight he couldn't breathe. He panted, fighting for air against the crushing weight.

"Will you calm yourself, Kanzo?" Der arched a brow.

Calm? He sat up, swinging his legs off the side of the bed. "Why would I not be calm?" He glanced at a chaotic medical and scowled. Flashes of memory returned. Of him sweeping the counters clear, flipping the bed, and destroying the room. Of the intense pain that lingered, fear and rage gripping his heart. Of the three males who'd tackled him to the floor. Of his Dar Eth, Ava—her fear darkening her stunning green eyes, and her hand reaching for his.

"Be calm." Der palmed his blaster, its yellow light blinking and drawing Kanzo's gaze.

"I am calm." He jumped to his feet and paused at Ulriq asleep on a bed. "How fairs the Supreme Commander?"

"He is almost healed. I would suggest you ask Prex what he has discovered. Threaten to destroy his lab if you are not pleased with his efforts." Der gestured to Kanzo to leave.

Kanzo grumbled as he strode to the Data Officer's lab. He requested entrance with no answer until the fourth time when the door opened to a glowering Prex.

"You will not touch anything." He slid into his seat in front of the multi-lit console. "Nerx has instructed Ksal to set our destination for Yithia. We suspect they took your

Dar Eth for reasons we have yet to determine." He pressed a button, and the display vid illuminated with Ava's last few minutes on the shuttle.

Kanzo ogled her image, mesmerized. Her exotic brown skin, her flowing black hair, her soft-looking lips, and her exquisite face.

"She is beautiful, Kanzo." Prex's words had him scowling at the data officer. "But something has upset her. Such a passionate creature."

Kanzo's gaze flashed to the vid in alarm. Upset? He studied his reaction to her touch, her flinch as if he'd struck her, then her pain-filled stillness. Alodon's balls. He'd harmed his Dar Eth without trying. Not considering how his actions might appear to her, he'd struggled to diminish the uncontrollable burn of lust she invoked in him. Fresh agony lanced through him now, but this was a different kind of pain, making his heart ache.

"I have drawn a schematic, laying out the positions of all in the shuttle at the time of the port." The sec-vid altered to display Prex's virtual model. "Why her? Lady Jack is with Danic, Lady Taylor with Mich, Lady Vicky was next to Aaro? It is illogical."

Kanzo studied the diagram, his gaze zigzagging across it. "Could this be a random targeting?" He rubbed a thumb across his jaw in thought.

"They would have scanned the shuttle, analyzed the life signs." Prex's fingers flew across the keys. "Ulriq's would have been the lowest of the Etterian males, due to his wounds."

"She sat beside Ulriq." Kanzo pointed at the diagram.

"They believed her to be Ulriq's Dar Eth." Prex grinned. "Look at her, Kanzo. Her hair is black, like ours."

"She looks nothing like our females." Kanzo frowned.

"Yes, but Yithians do not know this." Prex tapped his console. "This must mean they are escorting her to Yithia, to the royal court, and not the arena." He laughed, no doubt pleased at finding a logical solution. "Here are the results from the shuttle's sensors. They were not close enough for a shuttle-to-shuttle port. Our sensors would have alerted us." He gestured to a graph on his vid. "Here, the shield dipped. It appears as if they used its power to port her. It is ingenious." He tapped across the console again. "An external power surge would have alerted us, but not one from within the shuttle. I will reprogram the sensor sensitivity protocol. This will not occur again."

"Alodon's balls, Prex." Kanzo curled his fingers into fists and squeezed until the pain surpassed the constant ache inhabiting his very core. "I do not give a damn about preventing this. I *need* to find her."

"We are en route to Yithia. We can do nothing but wait." Prex's calm response gritted Kanzo's teeth.

"I apologize, thank you for the assistance." Kanzo rubbed his face.

Prex glanced at him. "I have commed Nerx. He is on his way."

Kanzo gestured to the display vid. "Please send her image to my O.D.I."

Prex narrowed his eyes for a moment before nodding. Nerx found Kanzo staring at his O.D.I.—a frozen image of Ava. He frowned at this breach of protocol before glancing at Prex.

Kanzo didn't care if violating data sharing protocol cost him a foot of honor. Maker, he'd lose another foot for Prex too, if need be. But having her image offered him some level of peace.

"Sub-Commander, this is what we have ascertained." Prex informed Nerx of his and Kanzo's findings.

"Good." Nerx commended Prex's efforts.

"With due respect, Sub-Commander, I would not have arrived at these conclusions without Kanzo's assistance."

Nerx's eyebrow arched at this, but he offered Kanzo a nod.

"We will need a plan for when we reach Yithia." Kanzo folded his arms across his chest, the image of Ava no longer activated.

"I would suggest you and Prex monitor all vids out of Yithia. Perhaps the Maker will assist us in her precise location." At Prex's deep sigh, Nerx faced him. "Is there an issue, Data Officer?"

"No, Sub-Commander." Prex glanced at his console. Kanzo stiffened. Neither he nor Prex would challenge their notoriously grumpy superior.

As soon as Nerx left them alone, Kanzo pulled a comfy closer. It was the mark of a true Etterian male, the strength to manipulate a magnetic-based chair. "Thank you, Prex."

"You make my life hell, and I vow, Kanzo..." Prex glared.

Kanzo smiled, shaking his head. "Find my Dar Eth, and I will be eternally in your debt."

"I have commed Data Officer Kemt. He is on board the battleship Phoenix patrolling Yithia. He is monitoring all transmissions and will comm any unusual vids." Prex split the display vid into two. "Here are the transcripts of the communications received, thus far."

Kanzo stared at line after line of dialogue in Yithian and scowled.

After hours of reading, he knew more about Yithian interaction than he had ever wanted to know. Inane chatter, operatives issuing strange orders, the back and forth of restocking, spaceship maneuvers, and gossip were a waste of time but expected. He struggled to keep his eyes open. A slap across his chest prevented him from slamming his forehead against the console.

"Go, rest. I will continue and comm you the moment I find anything of interest." Prex angled his jaw, determination in every line.

Kanzo swallowed his protest and rose. "Comm me in two hours." He stumbled to his unit in the barracks, crashing his face into his pillow.

As if moments later, a communication buzzed up his arm. Groaning, he rolled onto his back and activated his O.D.I. Over an hour had passed.

"Warrior Kanzo, the comm room, now." At Pilot Ksal's barked order, he jumped up, rubbed his face as if that would awaken him, and rushed out of his unit. Once he entered the communications room, he jerked to a halt at a raging supreme commander stomping back and forth.

"We were incorrect in our assessment. They were after Lady Jack," Prex said as Kanzo stood beside him. "They have taken her, as well."

"A temirian?" Kanzo arched a brow. With the shields utilized on the battleship, the only way anyone could port off or on was with a temirian device. Its purpose was to disrupt dampening shields, but it was expensive to purchase for casual use.

"Good, now that you are up to date, Kanzo, we leave within the hour," Ulriq said.

Kanzo had never seen his battle-bond this agitated. His face had darkened with anger, fear, and a pain he recognized.

Ulriq continued, "Prex has informed me that Phoenix's Kemt, under Supreme Commander Xan's command, has stumbled upon communication between a Yithian slave ship and the royal court."

"We suspect Lady Jack is heading for the arena." Prex leaned against a bulkhead, exhaustion in the circles under his eyes. "A unit will port down to rescue her, while I escort Kanzo to the Phoenix. With Supreme Commander Xan and his unit, we will rescue Lady Ava." He shut his eyes for longer than was needed before meeting Kanzo's gaze. "It should take five days to reach Mascroba, even with the scimitar at full fusion pulse. By then, we will know her location, Kanzo."

The scimitar was the perfect choice with sufficient capacity for eleven warriors. It had an engine room and ten small units, the same design as on an Etterian battleship. The officer's quarters remained unused if they utilized the craft for covert missions. It came with a well-stocked recreational room for longer than normal missions. Despite its size, the comm room was comparable to battleships, holding all the controls, navigational diagnostics, and battle weaponry to pilot such a ship.

A surge of energy burst through Kanzo. They were, at last, doing something, even if it meant spending five days in close confinement with six males. He rushed to his quarters, cleansed, dressed in another set of armor, and forced himself to eat something.

He was not the first in Docking Bay G. Nerx had taken to glaring at his males. Kanzo grinned, glad he did so to hasten them. With a shrug, he assisted with the refueling, the loading of ammunition and rehydrator fluid as well as the final checking of the oxygen tanks. His arms burned from the extensive effort and speed with which he performed some of these tasks. When his males performed second checks at each task completion, he accepted their palms pressed to his chest in a show of encouragement. Warmth saturated every pore at the sense of comradery around him.

Once onboard, Prex gestured to him to assume the co-pilot seat.

"You will continue to monitor the vids out of Yithia. As the pilot on this mission, I will focus on remaining undetected and keeping the scimitar at max speed."

"Acknowledged." Kanzo grinned and aligned the display vids allocated to him. They would stream Yithian data still arriving from Kemt. His main display held the dialogue transcripts, the other vids held various arena and newsworthy recordings. He maintained his focus, ignoring the bustle around him. None of that mattered. Finding Ava did.

Chapter Nine

A Cold Metallic Cell

Ava vacillated between awake and asleep, and only during a conscious moment did she realize they'd moved her to another cell. This one had a solid floor, smooth but still cold. The sickly yellow lights hidden in the bulkheads didn't illuminate much. She lay still, assessing her injuries. Her torso ached. She couldn't exert the energy to check whether there were bruises, but the area was sensitive to the touch. As were her swollen lip and cheek. Her ear throbbed—also not a good sign, but at least it had stopped bleeding. The added uncoiling of nausea in her gut was like the icing on the cake.

She sat up, shivering from the cold, enough for her to slip her arms through her sleeves to hug her body. Her fingers were like ice against her midriff, but it didn't matter, she was warmer from her efforts.

All things considered, she wasn't in too bad a condition for someone kidnapped by aliens. She chuckled, then burst into laughter so uncontrollable tears dribbled, stinging her bruises. Laughing tears turned into real tears, and she sobbed into her chest, unwilling to remove her arms from their warm cocoon.

As she sucked in deep breaths, trying to calm herself, she spied something at her feet. It looked like two sachets of water and two protein bars. She drew her arms through her sleeves again to pick up a bar. It squelched between her fingers like a solid tube of white. Her stomach gurgled, sharp twinges of pain announcing her hunger. She didn't know how much time had passed. Tearing the plastic-paper wrapping off with her teeth, she sucked the glop into her mouth and gagged. Bitterness coated her tongue, and when she tried to scrape it off, it clung like melted cheese. She threw the offensive 'bar' aside, then gaped as it dissolved, leaving droplets of white on the silver-gray floor. She made sure to drain every drop from the water sachets. The paper-plastic wrapping had the same stippled texture and might dissolve too. As she had guessed, they too disappeared.

She shuffled on her ass until she rested against the wall in the farthest corner from the door. The cell had an odd shape cell as if it was in an awkward section of the ship. The corner was sort of kinky but shielded her a little.

When she nestled in the angled corner, the cold of the metallic walls made her shiver. It was only temporary, like sitting on faux-leather in winter. She just had to be patient and not freeze to death while her body warmed the metal.

In an effort to distract herself, she wondered what the girls were up to? Had they returned home? Had Ulriq survived? Did Kanzo think of her? Her shoulders slumped. Her questions weren't helping to lighten her mood. As time ticked by, the past events settled in her mind, and the horror of her situation bloomed. Darkness engulfed her, tinging her vision until the pressure to cry forced her eyes shut.

Sucking in a shaky breath, she leaned on her experience when dealing with *difficult* situations. She compiled verbal letters to the children at her orphanage. Her voice sliced the suffocating silence and the muted hum of a far-off engine.

"Dearest Mikey, if I see you again, I *will* place a big whopper of a kiss on those ruddy cheeks of yours. I know you'll hate it and think it's a sissy thing, but I have loved teasing you. I hope you grow up to be a defender of the innocent, a champion to the meek." A tear slipped free, and she swiped it away, sniffing as she continued, "Sweet Lily, life has treated you badly, you more than the others. I have seen your scars." More tears trickled free. "But I love you, my fierce fighter. Help Tommy to make wise choices. You and I both know, he'll need you to survive in the big world, made bigger by evil sharks. I hope you never meet one."

By the time, she had addressed each child, her voice was hoarse, her corner warm, and her eyelids drooping. She didn't know how long it had been since the sharks had stolen her, but it didn't matter, not anymore. To survive, she knew what she needed to do, having done so too many times to count. The absolute hopelessness of her situation drove her toward her sanctuary.

Something whispered deep inside her that the next few days would be her most painful, worse than Mrs. Wheeler who had whipped her to within an inch of her life.

She drew in a deep breath and allowed her mind to drift, picturing rolling green hills, azure skies with fluffy clouds, and the warmth of the sun on her face. She was taller now, so too were the giant daisies and dandelions that brushed her fingertips as she meandered through the thigh-high lush green grass. Birds, alive with excitement, called to her to listen, to sing with them. Here, there was no time, no pain, and no sadness.

She crested a hill and gasped. Her safe zone had never had an ocean. Nor did the sharp cliff alarm her, for along it ran a path to the beach. Seagulls glided high, and the scent of the air was salty on her tongue. The flavor altered to acrid detergent. She gagged, then opened her eyes to gape at the white foam coating the cell floor. Was it meant to bathe her? Like she was a wild animal in a pen? She gritted her teeth and tucked her feet beneath her. The foam's bubbles popped but inches from her corner.

She scowled at its ability to disrupt her. Her body was still conscious of its surroundings. In her sanctuary, she didn't feel pain, not until she returned to reality. She'd fast learned the after-pain was more bearable than suffering through the ordeal.

Grumbling under her breath, she envisioned dandelions, picturing each petal, their vibrant yellow against their green stems, but found herself drifting off to sleep. She jerked awake and forced herself to return to her sanctuary. By the third attempt, she gave up and allowed sleep to claim her.

When she awoke, the foam had gone and another sachet and protein bar lay at her feet. She tossed the bar at the door and alleviated her bladder in the opposite corner of the cell. She pretended she was in a forest, squatting behind an ancient redwood, not in a cell.

When she had drip-dried, she faced her still-freezing cell. The sharks had to be cold-blooded or something to endure temperatures this cold. Cursing them, she harrumphed, grabbed the water sachet, and slid into her comfortable corner again.

A grating noise preceded the foam's spray, dragging her from her sanctuary. With the bubbles still coating the floor, the lighting flickered to white, and the door opened to Twyl and another shark.

"It defecates in the corner like an animal." Twyl curled his upper lip.

"She knows not how to activate the disposal receptacle." The other shark strode across the cell and touched a panel above her peeing spot.

Like something out of a science fiction novel, the door folded, and a cube slid out. Gasping, she staggered to her feet and joined him, assessing where he had pressed.

He demonstrated it once, studying her while she tested calling the toilet.

"Do you believe the king would appreciate such a gift?" The stranger faced Twyl.

She stilled, trying to act as if she wasn't eavesdropping. King? Shit, this was bad. She could count on one hand the number of historical kings who were good, decent men and not power drunk.

"An Etterian female is a rare find, Vlax. I believe the king will be most pleased." Twyl grinned, exposing his lethal-looking teeth.

"I do not see the attraction. She is too thin, and her skin does not glow." The shark named Vlax touched her arm then shuddered. "Her cold skin is pleasant to the touch but too dry." He stared at her upturned face. "I thought she would be taller, and...her eyes, Operative, they are *green*."

He stared at Twyl in alarm, well, she assumed it was that since his eyes grew larger with no other expression forming. At least their hisses no longer speared her brain. Small mercy.

Twyl shrugged. "She is a half-breed, Vlax."

Vlax stared at Twyl, curling his three fingers into a fist, before clasping his hands behind his back. "What is your name, female?"

Vlax didn't like Twyl. Not that the commonality would save her. "Ava," she hissed.

His snout twitched, straining the thick corded muscles in his A-line neck. "An Etterian name, but her accent is hideous."

"What do you expect from an interpreter?" Twyl shifted toward the door.

Relief softened the knot in her stomach. The thing in her ear was an interpreter and not a bomb. She was grateful for that bit of information.

"You will need to clothe her. What she is wearing is not suitable," Vlax said as if Ava was a dumb animal at a farmer's market.

"I am aware of this. Perhaps you could assist? After all, pleasing the king is your skillset." Twyl's left leg shook, as if he was eager to have done with her. The feeling was mutual.

"A harsh statement, Operative. Although, I shall accept the challenge." Vlax smirked, displaying his teeth, looking ravenous. She cringed. Were they cannibals? "Should you leave this cell, savage, will you attack me?"

"Me? The savage one?" She trembled as rage exploded through her. Biting her inner cheek was the only thing she could do to stop the tirade barreling up her throat. She flinched as Vlax raised his hand to discipline her.

"Do not beat the merchandise, Vlax. As it is, I had to waste med-patches on it." Twyl sauntered out, leaving her alone with Vlax.

He softened his voice. "I will ask you one more time, will you attack me?"

"No," she said from between her clenched teeth.

"If you test my patience, I will give the Operative a med-patch for every broken bone."

She swallowed past the lump in her throat. Broken bones?

He gestured, and she followed. What a coward she was. She should challenge him and get this over with.

The moment she stepped out of her cell, she scanned the passage. Two guards, also sharks, guarded various doors that were replicas of hers. Were there other cells, other prisoners? Vlax led her along passages, past scowling guards. The temperature dropped the further they went. By the time they entered a room, shivers racked her body with such violence her teeth chattered. His door shut with a finality that had her trembling for another reason. What had she agreed to? She smothered a snort. As if she had a choice.

Rubbing her arms, she studied his room. It wasn't much, but it was larger than her cell. One side held a ledge wide enough to sleep on. A desk dominated a wall, with fabrics strewn across it and a metallic chair in front of it.

"Remove your garments." His words confirmed her fears.

"What?" she squeaked.

"A med-patch so soon?" he lisped.

She held out a hand to stop him while she fiddled with the sash of her blouse. As much as she wanted to rid herself of her filthy clothing, she didn't want to be standing in front of him naked and vulnerable. With trembling fingers, she undid her sash and unwrapped the blouse, dropping it to the floor. She tugged off her shoes and tight leggings, shoving them with her foot. Digging deep into her sanctuary, she stood still, now in her bikini briefs, her breasts unbound.

"Everything?" she asked through her chattering teeth. Her nipples pebbled as goose-bumps spread across her body. She wrapped her arms around herself, shame adding to her quivering knees.

"No," the shark said. "I don't need to see more of you than I have to, savage." He draped fabrics over her, blessing her with seconds of warmth before tossing swaths of fabric aside. But minutes later, in a moment of frustration, he removed a sharp dagger and sliced the waistband of her panties. They fell to the floor in ruins. She bit her sore lip, trying to keep her horror inside. Cold tensed her shoulders while hunger twisted her insides. But neither compared with the humiliation claiming her soul. Within seconds, she basked in the warmth of her sanctuary's sun on her skin, the brush of daisy petals under her fingertips.

Sharp pain brought her back to reality. He had stabbed her with what looked like a pin.

"I am almost done, and you have behaved well." He leaned back and took his garment with him, leaving her naked and shivering. "You may cleanse." He gestured to the door behind her.

Cleanse? She bolted for the door. It slid open to a small bathroom complete with a toilet and shower. When she stepped into the shower cubicle, it activated before she had finished rubbing the panels looking for the on switch. Icy water drenched her, smothering her squeal. The temperature adjusted and hot water cascaded over her, warming her for the first time in days.

"Come, dress." Vlax hovered in the doorway, holding up a garment that looked like a hessian sack. It also offered warmth. Dripping wet, she stepped out of the spray and accepted the shirt, giving him a nod of thanks. She pulled it over her wet body and sighed. Yes, definitely warm. Her stomach chose that moment to make its abuse known.

Vlax scowled and stomped away from her. "What can you eat, female?"

Her head shot up. A part of her, the majority, warned her to distrust his kindness.

"Hot soup?" She winced. "I apologize. I don't know your foods…"

He tapped on a black glass surface, then out of nowhere, a gray bowl formed. Steam tendrils rose from the bowl—solid, with a thick rim, as if made from clay. He offered it to her. Chunks of something meaty floated in the yellow liquid, but she didn't care what manner of meat it was. It smelled amazing. She took a tentative sip. Salty, savory, with a decided fishy aftertaste filled her mouth. So good. She trembled, barely restraining the urge to pour the steaming nourishment down her throat. He studied her from his desk chair, so she sipped the soup until the bowl was empty.

"Thank you." She brought the bowl to him, relishing the heat exploding outward from her full belly.

He returned the bowl to the black glass where it faded. A cup formed, and the pungent odor of herbs assaulted her nose. He sat on the chair again.

His gaze remained fixed on her for a moment. He flashed his canines. "You are not Etterian." Folding his bulging arms across his massive chest with the cup gripped in one hand, he hissed-gaped as if he laughed. It sounded like an old man with breathing problems.

Oh, shit. She glanced at the door wondering how she could activate it or whether she could escape. When Vlax didn't move or speak, she peeked at him. "Will you tell the Operative?"

"No, savage, let him boil himself." Vlax shook his head. Boil? For a shark, the phrase made sense, like Earth's 'hang himself' adage. "Come, tell me about your planet." He gestured to his feet.

She sat. Despite his threats, he had yet to harm her. So she told him of blue skies, white clouds, indigo oceans, and the creatures within, except the sharks, lest she offended him. She mentioned the birds and the animals that were extinct, killed off by her ancestors.

"Are your females like you?" He fondled a lock of her damp hair.

"No, we can be stubborn, opinionated, brave, and silly. Our personalities vary as do yours?" She shrugged. "I knew of other species in our universe, but until a few days ago, I'd never met an Etterian or your kind."

He released her hair and brought the cup to his mouth. Taking a long swallow, he fixed his gaze on her. He twirled the cup in his three-fingered hand. "Yithia has three suns. We are forever in daylight. Nothing like your singular moon and sun. We live underwater, where it is the coolest, and venture out onto the small land surfaces for short periods of time."

She gaped. Three suns? And yet they lived underwater? In caves? She asked as much. Vlax hiss-laughed. "No, oceans cover Yithia."

That made sense. If Earth had less landmass, humans might have learned to live underwater too. "Do you farm or mine minerals? On what is your economy based?"

He raised an eyebrow, one side of his lips curling. "We export some minerals, but our biggest token-generation comes from our arena. Yithians love to gamble, and so do other worlds."

"Arena? Like gladiators? Fighters?"

"Many prisoners on this ship will die in the arena. The most lucrative opponent was a human female."

"Was?" She stilled. "Did she die?"

"No, she escaped with the help of Etterians. It is why we seek more Earthian females."

"Like Jack," Ava offered information, hoping Vlax would remain forthcoming.

He frowned. "Jack?"

"Yes, my sister. They were after her but got me instead. Am I not destined for the arena?"

"No, savage. Your black hair has saved you."

"It has?" She captured a lock, then asked the question on the tip of her tongue. "Aren't you tempted to sell me to the arena?"

He drained then stared at the bottom of his cup. His eyes narrowed. "No. I have waited many solar revolutions for Twyl to receive his just rewards. But you are an innocent, a tool he will abuse for his gain. I will prepare you, and should Calzantu see fit to bless you, then so be it. Your life may be a luxurious one if you please the king."

She grimaced. Spreading her thighs for a shark was not for her. Then again, maybe that wasn't what Vlax meant. "How do I please the king when you don't find me attractive?"

He hiss-laughed and patted her on her head with a stiff hand. This was the alien who'd threatened to break her bones. And he would, if she misbehaved, attacked him, or was rude to him. Of that, she had no doubts.

"As an Etterian female, our King Urio would not kill you for fear of your death starting a war."

"But then the operative won't boil." Her lips twitched as if she could find amusement in her situation.

Vlax grinned. "Never fear, he will. Once the king realizes he was deceived." He rose and gestured to a pile of blankets he tossed on the floor.

She climbed to her feet and inched across to it. Feeling like a puppy but not caring since the blankets promised warmth, she lowered herself onto the pile. A click preceded the weight of a metal collar, ice-cold against her throat. Stunned, she gaped as he clipped a chain to her new jewelry and the end of the chain to a ring in the bulkhead.

"I do not trust you, savage. And I do so love my sleep. Lack of sleep makes me irritable and irritable me breaks bones, so try not to disturb me."

She nodded, unable to say anything over the lump in her throat. She shouldn't have expected decency from her kidnapper. Worse, she had revealed she wasn't Etterian and told him about Jack. She was such a stupid gullible idiot. Regardless of his distrust, the pile of blankets provided the best sleep she'd had in days.

Chapter Ten

Etterian Scimitar Yakin
En route to Mascroba, Yithia
The Comm Room

"WE ARE MAKING GOOD time, just two days out." Ulriq paused behind Prex and Kanzo sitting in front of the console. "Have you found anything yet?"

Kanzo straightened his slumped shoulders, slicing agony across his back. "I have translated enough Yithian to not need the O.D.I."

Ulriq studied him. "How is the Ethera?"

"Bearable. It helps that I have her image." Kanzo activated his O.D.I. to call up the sec-vid.

"Is Jack on there?" Deep need saturated Ulriq's voice.

A similar ache, constant, insistent, registered in Kanzo.

"No, I sent him only the minutes before Ava's phasing." Prex hastily punched on the console keys and the sec-vid from the shuttle appeared on the display vid.

Ulriq's breath caught, and he barely hid a shudder. "You two, go rest." His tone brooked no argument.

They left their supreme commander in the comm room alone with Jack's shuttle images. Kanzo strode to his quarters, an exact replica of those on the *Kushin*. He cleansed, resting his forehead on the white tiles, letting the water soothe him. Once done, he spread out onto his bed, naked, his right arm bent behind his head as he stared at Ava's holographic image on his left forearm.

"Play," he said, and the vid continued, showing her misery. Yet despite her pain, she had called to him, had trusted him to save her. That alone filled him with bright, welcoming hope.

He analyzed her expressions, concluding she believed he hated her, that he didn't want her. Every time he reviewed the vid, he vowed to himself that the moment she was in his arms, he would make her see the truth. He focused on the vid again until the part where she called his name.

"Pause." The vid froze. Having her face near was the only way he could sleep. As if her image could ever replace the wealth of sensations holding her generated. He ached for her, needed to scent her, to touch her despite the pain it would evoke. Pain *and* pleasure, he reminded himself.

"Kanzo," Prex boomed.

Kanzo bolted into a sitting position, blinking at Prex who reached across and deactivated his O.D.I.

"Good, you are awake. Kemt has found something."

Kanzo was on his feet in an instant, yanking on his military pants before pulling on a long-sleeved tunic. He tugged on his boots and rushed after Prex. "How long was I asleep?"

"Six hours."

"Alodon's balls, it felt like seconds." He rubbed his face, his eyes gritty. "What did—?"

"You need to see it." Prex slid into the seat.

Ulriq stood to the side with his arms folded across his chest.

Kanzo peered at the text on the display vid. A Yithian operative bore a gift for King Urio and requested an audience. When the Emissary questioned the gift, the words 'Etterian female' stood out. The Emissary doubted the validity of the gift, so the operative communicated an image.

"Maker." Kanzo groaned at the image of Ava before him.

She wore nothing but sashes, strips of fabrics in various colors, flowing down from her hips to her bare toes. The fabric was translucent, hinting at her toned legs and the dark curls at the juncture of her thighs. Another sash crisscrossed her chest, barely covering her breasts, the undersides visible as were her nipples and her taut stomach. They had left her hair unbound, and it flowed around her like a black waterfall, the curls wrapping around her upper arm, and over one breast.

"She is beautiful," Prex said for the second time.

The image disappeared from the display vid and a buzz up Kanzo's arm confirmed receipt. He managed to nod his thanks, his body too tense for him to command it to do anything let alone speak.

"The king has accepted the gift," Prex said, buying Kanzo time to rein in his arousal.

"At least the royal court is her confirmed destination," Ulriq said in a bored tone. "Confirm Kanzo's transfer for tomorrow and inform Supreme Commander Xan to prepare."

Etterian Scimitar, Iqiniso
En route to Issneen, the Royal City, Etteria
The Officer's Quarters

"Truth, Barro?" Prince Citus, the Etterian Ambassador, grunted at the display vid communication from his friend, the Ambassador of Maloid. The yellow-skinned bastard was grinning at him as if he had won a lifetime stay at Iphara, the paradise island on Yithia. His ever-swaying tentacles distracted Citus, making it harder for him to focus on the conversation. He glanced at his O.D.I. to rein in his thoughts. He should be used to conversing with all manner of species when he traveled between planets for negotiations, festivals, and council meetings.

"I insist you veer your course in my direction, Citus. This is something neither of us can pass up." He gestured at his surroundings, which were opulent even for Yithian standards. "You are a few hours out. Urio is to receive the gift today." The male chuckled, the sound rasping and the norm for Maloidians. In his excitement, the dark markings across his forehead and tentacles lightened. Citus smiled. It wasn't often Barro was this animated. "I shall secure it for you. You can reimburse me later, along with a favor. An

Etterian favor is worth far more than a shipment of Omeika." Barro grinned at the vid. "Do not disappoint me."

Citus blinked at the blank display and sighed. Whatever this was, it had better be legitimate. With a curse, he instructed his pilot to alter the Iqiniso's course for Yithia, at full fusion pulse. The delay would put him a day behind schedule.

He needed to visit Etteria, to feel the suns' rays on his face, inhale the sweet-scented hahyt blossoms. That he missed his homeworld was no surprise since he'd spent the last six months in the bowels of a planet plagued by cold electrical storms on the surface.

The Maloidians lived underground, in damp caverns their large and loud mechanical fans barely managed to aerate. The royal chambers were just as damp and foul-smelling. Thank the Maker, he at least had his scimitar to escape to. But he had to admit, he was fond of the elderly queen, Alllero, and he suspected she had a soft spot for him too. She often squeezed his forearm, which was a strange thing for her to do. She would do it then rasp her laughter. He smiled at the memory.

"For Etteria." He bounded up and activated his O.D.I., prepared to send his brother a message. He paused. One day's delay to reach Etteria? Did he need to communicate it? He grunted and cleansed instead.

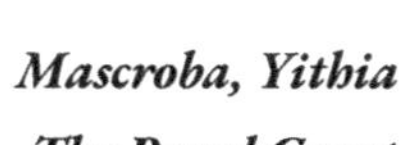

Mascroba, Yithia
The Royal Court

Ava trailed Operative Twyl, conscious of every step she took. The sashes swirled around her, revealing her bare thighs as she sashayed after the ponderous Twyl. She was more exposed than in her bikini. Having spent the last few days with eccentric Vlax, she understood why he had clothed her in this...indecent, pornographic garment. It was all to draw the attention of one alien, the Maloidian Ambassador, Barro. According to Vlax, he was the only male who could save her. So, she showed Twyl deference, despite the chain he clasped in his three-fingered grip.

Silence descended as soon as the large doors opened onto the Yithian royal court. Ice cold air greeted her, and she shivered as goosebumps raced across her skin. The hall was a dark cavern and she the lamb. Struggling to swallow, she fought the urge to tug at her collar. Slipping a finger under it forced her to realize it wasn't too tight, yet the sensation persisted.

The dragging of the metallic chain on the floor parted the crowd as Twyl led her toward the throne. The court quieted until the clinking echoed off the ebony stone walls. She stared ahead, her shoulders back, her head held high as she pushed through the humiliation. Welcome heat traveled down her neck to her collarbones. She shouldn't be embarrassed. In Vlax's quarters, he'd worked around her naked form, attaching diaphanous strips onto a wide waistband. He'd shown her his masterpiece, commanded her to move, to swirl the fabric with glimpses of her nudity beneath. Her unrestrained breasts had bounced with each step she took. The seductive sway of her hips, the ripple of muscle along her thighs as the strips danced around her legs had delighted Vlax. He'd compared her to some sea creature she couldn't pronounce.

Her future was unknown, and she sent up another prayer that the alien king was in a good mood. Twyl paused in front of the dais and kneeled. As Vlax had instructed her to do, she stood tall, awaiting Twyl's command. He yanked on the chain. The metal collar bit into her neck. She swallowed a cry and lowered herself to her knees, remembering to keep her eyes downcast.

"This is an Etterian female?" King Urio's voice reached the farthest corners of the hall, resonating across the silence.

"A half-breed, my king," Twyl said to the polished stone floor.

"A half-breed? In what way?" The king thundered toward her, his heavy steps as loud as his voice.

Panic clawed at her throat. Curling her fingers into her palm, she embedded her nails, hoping the sharp stings would calm her.

"Rise, half-breed Etterian female." The king waved a massive arm.

She rose, thankful she could do so in one smooth motion.

"You may look upon me," he commanded.

She met his gaze. Before her stood a super-large shark, a Megalodon, in a royal cloak. She tamped down a chuckle that might get her killed. One did not laugh at royalty, even if he was alien.

"Green eyes? They are not Etterian blue, yet the green is as unusual. Your name?"

Her shoulders dropped an inch. "Ava, Great Illustrious King Urio," she said as Vlax had instructed. She waited with bated breath for the king's next question. Vlax had asked she not reveal her origins, to allow him time to escape. He didn't wish to boil with Twyl when the truth became known. And for the kindness she had shown him, she would wait.

"I accept this gift, Operative Twyl." The king took the chain from Twyl's fingers and yanked her behind him as he climbed the dais to his throne. As he assumed his chair, he gestured to his feet. She slid to the floor, displayed her legs, bared her thighs, and arched her back while sitting up straight as Vlax had taught her.

Rolling her lips inward, she tried to smother a snort. She could just imagine her attempt to follow Vlax's instructions only to look like a spastic marionette. Sitting on the cold stone floor pebbled her nipples and turned her fingertips blue. She shivered, then the cold touch of the king on her bare upper arm snapped her attention to him. He gestured to an emissary who spread pillows on the floor for her to sit upon. She shifted across, thankful for the kind gesture. She offered the king a small nod of thanks. Vlax had warned. To flash her teeth at a Yithian was to invite sexual relations. She didn't want that, just the thought of it had her skin crawling.

She listened to the first few petitions of he said, she said. They were trivial for the most part. After a while, boredom set in, and she spent the time guessing what issue each one would bring as they approached the king.

"Do you not approve, Ava?" the king asked her. Her head shot up, and she realized that all awaited her response. She blushed and darted her gaze at the king in panic. "You are free to speak."

"It's...petty," she whispered. He jerked back and his obsidian eyes widened. Should she have remained silent? What else could she have said?

"The Gift of Ava said, 'It's petty,'" the royal announcer said, loud enough for the court to hear.

Her cheeks burned. So much for softly-spoken.

"Continue..." King Urio wiggled his long fingers.

"He said this, she said that, make them stop saying nasty things to me," Ava mimicked in a whine, "...like children."

The king blinked at her. A loud noise erupted from him, a hissing-laugh made even more bombastic by his sheer size.

"Children?" And he laughed again. "I assume Xeus handles them differently?"

She frowned. Zeus? As in the god in Greek Mythology? Well, she supposed he must have...or did? "A king should have an adviser, one who hears each complaint and brings the crucial ones to the king's attention." She sighed, wishing the floor would just crack open and swallow her. How many enemies had she just made? She had called their issues petty.

"And what should I look for in an adviser?" If it wasn't for his huge canine-displaying smile, she might not have taken the time to advise him. At the sight of his pointed teeth, she glanced at her hands. Eye contact might encourage him. She swallowed. Shit, she hoped he wasn't interested in her that way.

"A trusted friend, someone who doesn't want your throne, power, or wealth?" She twisted a sash between her twitching fingers. "Someone who is honest with you even when you don't want them to be."

"A rare find indeed," the king mused.

She didn't know if he meant her or this adviser he needed, so opted for the latter. "True friends always are." A pang struck, twisting her gut. She missed her family, the ache in her chest growing at the thought of never seeing them again.

"Gift of Ava said, 'True friends always are,'" the announcer said.

She glared at him, wishing he would shut up.

"Etteria would pay dearly for your return." King Urio's smile widened even further.

Oh, shit. Her gaze shot up to meet his, alarm now apparent. That smile, could it mean greed, as well? Vlax never mentioned that it could mean both, but judging by Urio's words, perhaps it did. She hoped so.

"My apologies, my king. I'm a half-breed and a dishonored one." She gestured to her hair, as Vlax had instructed. Etterians measured their honor by the length of their hair. Since hers brushed the middle of her back, she wasn't valued.

"It is true, my king." A yellow alien man with flowing tentacled hair bowed before Urio. "I, myself, would be willing to purchase her from you."

"Barro," the King roared. "You state she is not wanted by Etteria just to lower her purchasing price." He lifted a thick strand of her hair to toy with. "Out of curiosity, what would she be worth to you?"

"Ten thousand tokens," the male said without hesitation.

The king dropped her hair and leveled his black gaze on the Maloidian. "Throw in your Scimitar, and we have a deal."

"*Isus* was a gift from King Xeus." Barro glanced at Ava, then away, but not before she caught a slight smirk. "Very well, King Urio. The *Isus* is yours."

"Halt." Urio pushed off his throne, leaning his bulk over a calm Barro. "You have never wanted to part with such a ship before. Why now?"

"I have grown bored with it, King Urio. Is it a deal?" Barro met and held the Yithian king's gaze.

"Yes."

"So states the king," the announcer said.

Barro held out his hand, and the king handed over the chain. Barro tugged on it, and she rose to her feet, keeping her gaze down. She trailed him under the watchful gaze of the court, the chain once more dragging on the stone floor.

"May Alllero shine upon you, my king," the Maloidian said in parting.

"And on you."

The crowd erupted into a cacophonous chatter moments before the large doors sealed them out.

Chapter Eleven

Etterian Scimitar, Yakin
En route to Mascroba, Yithia
The Communications Room

Mascroba, City of Yithia, the official seat of the Royal Court and the arena was two hours out. They were close enough to receive arena vids but not near enough to port. The unit had witnessed Jack and Warrior Teric's performance in the arena. That the sogair had almost killed her was something no one dared to mention. The dark red creature had sprinted into the arena, snarling and hissing, its razor-sharp teeth dripping saliva. Huge in size, it dwarfed Jack who'd raised an Earth weapon, small and black in her tiny hands.

Kanzo was certain this was her final moments. Relief flooded them all when she and Teric walked out of the arena, but Ulriq still trembled with barely contained emotion. Kanzo had given his battle-bond a forearm clasp, Eth to Eth. "Breathe," was all he'd said.

Ulriq had nodded and pressed his palm to Kanzo's shoulder.

Now the Scimitar was quiet, deathly so, as Prex hurtled them toward the battleship Phoenix.

"Anything new on the vids?" He handed Kanzo a giyua juice.

"I have not verified the latest received." He activated the transmission display vid and flicked through the titles while sipping the tart beverage. In bold, the text leaped at him. He forced himself to read it, not that he wanted to. Operative Twyl's Well-Received Gift. His finger twitched as he drew in a shuddering breath, gathering his control and strength. He double-tapped the title and waited the mere seconds it took to download.

He froze, unable to move, to breathe when Ava trailed the operative. The chain scraped across the floor. He scowled, anger curling his fingers at their audacity. She wasn't a gift, a prize, or a slave. Despite her restraints, she glided across the court, regal, head high, as a queen would. She wore the same garment as in her image. With every move she made, more of her nudity was revealed. Her long legs parting the sashes with each step stuttered his heartbeat. He was semi-aroused since meeting her. With her swaying hips, bouncing breasts, and arching back, he was harder than the Fuyra rock Etteria mined. His breath came in gasps, his heart pounded in his ears, deafening him, while hot, scorching pleasure shot through his veins.

"Ambassador Barro has her now." Prex punched the keys on the console sending Kanzo the vid. The male violated protocol on Kanzo's behalf, but what did it matter when everyone had seen his Dar Eth so...enticing. He shivered and reached for his juice, grateful for the cool liquid on his tongue. "Phoenix is on standby, one hour." Prex faced him. "Supreme Commander Xan will negotiate with Barro for her release. This is much better than stealing her from Urio." That Prex had not used Urio's title implied his opinion of the Yithian king.

"Scimitar *Eshima* to scimitar *Yakin*, acknowledge," a male voice came across the secure comm.

"Scimitar *Yakin*, Data Officer Prex, acknowledging." He grinned at the console. "We were not expecting a response so soon."

"A female in danger requires our full attention. We are in porting range, please lower your shields for transfer."

"Shields lowered." Prex rested his palm on Kanzo's shoulder. "Bring her home, Kanzo."

Kanzo grinned, eager to find and claim her. Within seconds, his body tingled as he teleported to Supreme Commander Xan's scimitar.

"Warrior Kanzo, welcome aboard the *Eshima*," Xan said with a forearm clasp, all the while staring at his ice-blue eyes.

"Thank you, Supreme Commander Xan. I appreciate your efforts to assist in this rescue."

"She is exquisite, Warrior Kanzo. What species is she?" Xan's voice held awe.

Kanzo inhaled sharply. Xan's words confirmed they'd also seen her so...exposed. "She is a human from Earth." He addressed the males on board. "Set your O.D.I. for Earth English, it is the only language Ava speaks."

They did as instructed.

"Data Officer Kemt." A male introduced himself with a forearm clasp. "Every male will give their life for your lady, Warrior Kanzo."

Kanzo nodded. "Thank you for your assistance, Kemt. Prex and I appreciate it."

The male resumed his seat at the console.

"We are attempting to communicate with Ambassador Barro, yet he continues to elude us." Xan's anger at the delay rattled his cheeks, his jaw clenched.

"Is he trustworthy, Supreme Commander?" Ava had been in the Ambassador's yellow clutches longer than Kanzo preferred.

"Yes—"

"Supreme Commander, Prince Citus is sending an urgent comm," Kemt said.

Xan crossed to stand in front of the display vid just as Citus's features appeared. "My prince."

Citus frowned. "I am here on strange business for which I cannot anticipate the outcome. Be on standby for a possible collection."

Xan arched a brow. "Would this be a hasty collection as per the time you cost me my favorite scimitar?"

"Truth, Xan, you cannot even recall the name of this favorite scimitar," Citus chuckled.

Xan grunted at this, though a smile did twitch his lips.

Kanzo smiled, sensing that the escape had been entertaining. Perhaps a story for another time.

Xan mumbled a curse, before continuing, "Regardless, we are in a rescue situation. Might I suggest you delay your collection?"

"Unacceptable. Collect me first," Citus said.

"Dar Eths take priority, as per our law, my prince." This time, Xan chuckled.

Citus gaped. "Dar Eth?" he whispered.

Xan flicked a hand. "Kanzo, come forward."

Kanzo obeyed and stepped in front of the display vid. He leveled his gaze on the prince. "Prince Citus."

A few minutes passed as Citus blinked at him, his face shoved an inch from the vid. Kanzo fought the urge to twitch like a young warrior under Base Commander Remi's stern gaze.

"Very well, I shall attend to this issue planetside, and once your Dar Eth is on board then send an escort." Citus scowled at Xan through the display vid. "And I expect a full debriefing post-rescue. Include Warrior Kanzo and his Dar Eth."

"Always a pleasure," Xan said to the blank screen. "Comm the Ambassador again and locate his chambers. We might need to surprise him with a visit."

Chapter Twelve

Mascroba, Yithia
The Svanon Zone

THE MALOIDIAN AMBASSADOR'S CHAMBERS was art personified. The smooth floor looked like polished volcanic rock. The walls were jagged cliff faces, lined with depictions of colorful flora, exotic and odd. The sky near the ceiling was a brilliant purple with bright zigzags of lightning. And the lighting was a deep purple splattered with pinpoint lights. As Ava spun to admire the décor, the black chairs, tables, and cabinets, her chain clinked, reminding her she wasn't alone.

"How did you manage to convince them you are Etterian?" Ambassador Barro shut the metal door to his chambers.

She squeaked and glanced at him, panic and fear exploding nausea in the pit of her stomach. Shit, she had failed. Running her gaze over the yellow alien, she searched for kindness around his eyes, in what expressions she recognized. The constant smile was a ruse. No one was this jovial all the time.

"Do not be alarmed. You are safe with me. I commed the Etterian ambassador the moment I saw your image, thinking you were Etterian. He is en route to collect you. Since you are not Etterian, let us see what he has to say." He rasped in laughter. "Is Ava your name?"

"It is." She shared a close-mouthed smile, careful not to encourage a more intimate interaction. His skin shimmered like a rubber chicken's. Smothering a giggle, she forced herself to breathe, to relax. Vlax had been correct to lead her toward this ambassador. She hadn't trusted the Yithian to honor his word, but she was delighted he had. Here, before her, was another alien offering her refuge. If he had reached out to an Etterian, then there was hope she would make it home. If said Etterian led her to Kanzo, then she would have the opportunity to apologize to him for her misjudgment.

"Twyl decided I was an Etterian half-breed and…" She shrugged.

"And you thought it wise to let him continue believing so?" Barro studied her face, though what he searched for, or whether he found it, she couldn't say.

She swallowed past the lump in her throat. Those first few days had been hell.

"Your delicate features are expressive, more so than an Etterian's. Yet I sense an underlying strength beneath your softness." He tipped her chin up, urging her to meet his solid black eyes. "A captive has no sway with a Yithian operative, yet here you stand, having escaped the clutches of an operative and a king. What planet are you from?"

"I am a human woman from Earth." She smiled. "But I can't direct you to find it. Humans haven't traversed farther than our galaxy."

He released her chin and gestured to a chair.

"I'm sorry I cost you so much." She slid onto the chair, layering the strips of fabric to cover her better.

"I am certain of my reimbursement," Barro rasped. "Your attempts at modesty are pointless, ommia. Why do you bother when all of Yithia, the colonies, and any outlying ships have seen your image?"

"What?" she squeaked, winced, then squeezed her eyes shut.

"A prize such as yourself would need advertising, would you not agree?"

As an Etterian half-breed, she was a prize. As a hairdresser from Earth? No, there was nothing prizeworthy about her.

She settled her gaze on him, fascinated by the gentle sway of his yellow tentacles. His features were human, in that he had a mouth, a bump for a nose, and two solid-black, pupilless eyes. A swirl on the sides of his head demarcated his ears, embedded in the thick, fleshy tentacles patterned with black markings.

"I understand your garment is uncomfortable, however, for the sake of appearances I need you to remain as such."

She lowered her gaze to the chain coiled at her feet. "Including the chain?"

He flashed an apologetic smile. When his door chimed a few minutes later, he indicated the floor at his feet. Appearances, he said. Huffing, she slid into place, assuming the same posture as at Urio's feet. Shit. She stiffened, hating having to play the role.

If it bought her freedom, she had to muscle through it.

Over the next hour, Barro had many visitors, all to ogle her. Such a rare find, an Etterian half-breed, might have saved her ass, but not from being stared at like a caged animal. His visitors touched her arms, legs, and played with her hair. They even poked her chest, tweaked her nipples, looked at her teeth, and not in a gentle way. Clenching one hand, she dug her nails into the palm, the pain something for her to focus on. Unable to bear the touching a moment longer, she slipped into her sanctuary.

Tension drained from her as the warm sunlight kissed her upturned face. Exotic fragrances carried on the breeze, and her apple tree drooped under the weight of its fruit.

She raised a hand, undulating it through the cool waters of a nearby stream. Tiny rainbows formed where the waterfall plunged into the pool. Shaking the droplets off her fingers, she touched her neck and along her collarbone, sighing with pleasure.

"Lady Ava, you are the most irritatingly beautiful creature I have ever known."

She ignored the rasped words carried on the breeze and dipped her fingers into the pool again, tempted to lower her feet into its enticing depths. A caress not her own ran along her jaw. Her heart leaped. Kanzo was here? She smiled and raised her face to meet Barro's gaze. Disappointment slammed into her, stripping her of her hard-fought joy, and she gasped, scanning the empty room.

"Where do you go?" Barro's dark gaze traveled her face. "Where is this place you dream about?"

"It's my sanctuary." She frowned. How did he know about it? Were Maloidians mind readers? "I apologize, Ambassador, I didn't mean to offend you."

He waved a dismissive hand. "Is there anything you need, food, a beverage?"

At the mention of a beverage, her bladder twinged. She dipped her chin to her chest, plucking at a strip. "The ladies' room?" At his puzzled frown, she sifted through her memories. What would Barro call the toilet? "Your cleansing room?"

With a smile, he pointed to a door nearest the metal entrance.

"Thank you." She rose to her feet and looped the chain around her forearm. Bursting into a run, she hurried across to the door, her sashes tangling between her legs.

CITUS STARED AT THE carved Maloidian-steel door—a symbol of Maloid's strength—his fingers twitching against his thigh. He didn't have time for this nonsense. The door slid open, and he slipped through the growing gap, too impatient to wait. Striding across the stone floor, he did not spare the room more than a cursory glance.

"If it is a jewel or a silk garment, there will be hell, Barro," Citus said in Galactic as he halted before him.

"Oh, my friend, my dear, dear Citus, come sit with me and see." Barro gestured to the chair beside him with a clear view of the room.

Citus folded his long frame into the chair and waited. He studied the room, trying to ascertain what Barro expected him to see. "New furnishings?"

"Patience, Citus." Barro grinned but didn't look away from the cleansing room's door.

Citus narrowed his gaze on it.

"For this, I demand twenty thousand tokens, a new Scimitar, and one favor."

Citus twisted to glare at Barro. "Twenty? Are you insane? What could possibly be worth so much?"

"Patience, Citus."

Sighing, he faced forward again. He released the chair when he dug his clenched fingers into the dark wood. Barro's good humor added to the tension in Citus's shoulders. Seconds from leaping off the chair to leave, the cleansing room's door opened. He froze.

His breath hitched as he ran his gaze over her. Maker, she was exquisite. Her delicate frame, the mid-back fall of her brown-black hair, the soft glow of her skin. She smiled as she hurried across to him, the strips of fabric parting and trailing her like the tail of a celestial comet. His nostrils flared as he inhaled her scent, foreign yet tantalizing.

"What...is she?" he whispered, not hiding his awe, despite knowing it would cost him.

Barro grinned. "She is a human from Earth." He jumped up and took the chain from her hand, 'tugging' her behind him. Her smile for Citus glowed brighter, sheer joy rolling off her. Her green eyes sparkled, as well. The sight of it filled Citus's chest with unexpected warmth. "Lady Ava, this is Ambassador Citus."

"You're here," she hissed in Yithian before glancing around the chambers. "Is Kanzo with you?"

Barro stilled and snapped his head toward her.

"Kanzo?" Citus laughed. Alodon's balls, what were the odds? "Tell me, milady, Barro says you are from Earth?"

"Yes."

At Barro's scowl, Citus swallowed his chuckle. With how extensively Etterians traveled, the Maloidian Ambassador shouldn't be surprised that Citus knew of the planet this lovely creature called home. Nor did his friend know that he daily sifted through new planetary additions to their annals.

"And are there many females on your homeworld?"

"Oh, yes, millions," she said.

Millions? Excitement coursed through him, burning along his veins. He struggled to hide it from his too-observant token-hungry friend. As Kanzo's Dar Eth, she and her kind promised the salvation Etteria desperately needed. Wait until he told Xeus of this.

"Deal." Citus smiled at a gaping Barro. "The favor cannot be monetary or an export product from any planet. And I will not kill anyone for you."

Barro's eyes widened, and a pout formed. "No bargaining, just like that? I was hoping you would negotiate."

Citus gripped the Maloidian's forearm. "You do appreciate a good negotiation, but alas, I am behind schedule and due in Issneen."

"I have this feeling I am the loser in this bargain," Barro grumbled.

"I would suggest you have a medic look at that." Citus grinned as he punched into his O.D.I.

Barro scowled before facing a joyful Ava who danced on her toes, swishing her ribbons with *damu*-like abandon.

Chapter Thirteen

Mascroba, Yithia
The Svanon Zone

"Prince Citus demands we attend to him now," Kemt said to Xan. "He states that he has the salvation of Etteria, and she has Ferusi-green eyes."

Kanzo's head shot up as he paused in the punching of the wall mount, his physical exertion a desperate attempt to calm the Ethera. They waited to port. Frustration, anger, impatience, and the Ethera drove him. He *needed* her.

"Ava?" Kanzo coughed to clear the catch in his voice.

Xan held up a hand and tapped into his O.D.I. "Lady Ava. We have clearance to port down."

A male tossed Kanzo a cloth to wipe the sweat off his body. He hurried to do so before donning his military chest armor. They phased into the city, just outside a carved metal door. On either side were long, elaborate corridors. The air was thick with Yithia's oppressive heat. Only visiting dignitaries lived above the water.

Xan scowled and double verified they had the correct coordinates. He requested entrance. Once the door clicked open, he pushed in, striding toward where Citus and Ambassador Barro sat.

Kanzo trailed the supreme commander, a bounce to his step, his fingers twitching in anticipation. He focused on Prince Citus, glanced at the Maloidian then froze mid-stride. He couldn't miss the female at Barro's feet, though he did scowl at the sight of her chain and collar still in place.

"Ava." Kanzo rushed across the chamber as she leaped to her feet and ran toward him. He slowed to a halt gaping at her garment parting, her joyful smile, and the scraping of the chain dragging behind her. She stopped inches from him and raised her fingers as if to touch him then shyly pulled away.

"Hello, Kanzo," she greeted in Yithian.

He jerked at her language choice then ran an appraising gaze over her, mesmerized by her garments, by the parts of her body it emphasized and revealed. The images weren't a true reflection. She was breathtaking. He didn't know what to do first, hug her, kiss her, confess what she meant to him? So he took care of the irritation.

With his hands, he snapped the collar off her neck and tossed it to the floor. Whisps of her unbound hair stroked his hands, so he succumbed and buried his fingers in the curls behind her ears. He cupped her face with his palms. A deep shudder ripped through his body as intense joy burned through him, summoning a grin.

"Ava." His voice was too hoarse, but he didn't care. He spoke in Yithian, planning to teach her how to swap to her language at a later stage. "Are you well?"

"Yes, Kanzo." She rested her hands on his upper arms. Her green gaze met his.

Enthralled by the color, he allowed himself to fall into their depths. Why did she look at him like this? Didn't she blame him for her kidnapping? For not rescuing her sooner? But she seemed pleased to see him. Hope evoked something deep within him. As he stared at her, she darted her gaze away, her cheeks warming under his palms.

He wrapped his arms around her and crushed her to him before lifting her off the floor. Her weight was negligible as he buried his face in her neck. He drew in a deep breath to capture her scent and trap it within his lungs. Touching the skin of her bare back, he groaned at the softness just under his fingertips.

"You look tired." Her eyes glistened with unshed tears. She caressed his face with the feathering of her fingers, brushing along his jaw before slipping around his neck in a more intimate position.

He chuckled at her observation. "I am tired, but I am at peace."

"Peace?" She played with his hair at the nape of his neck.

"I have you in my arms, Ava," he said.

Her eyes widened. He'd been correct in his assessment. She believed he didn't want her, didn't want to hold her, to touch her. The silly female. Her hair formed a curtain around them, affording them some privacy. Without pre-thought, he feathered his lips across hers. The feel of her softness and her breath merging with his surged a tremor through him.

She gasped, but her eyelashes fluttered on a blissful sigh.

He wanted to kiss her again, to taste her. She cupped his face and kissed him just as tenderly as he had done to her. At her unexpected initiative, he tightened his arms, splayed his fingers across her bare back, and buried his face in her neck to inhale her scent again. He pressed an open-mouthed kiss to the pulse just below her jaw then dusted kisses over to her mouth.

"What is the meaning of this, Citus?" Barro's question intruded on Kanzo's moment. The Maloidian darted glances between Xan and Citus, expecting one of them to answer him.

"What's the matter?" Ava pressed her cheek to Kanzo's. "Why is the ambassador so angry?" She glanced at the Maloidian before frowning at Kanzo. "I can't understand him."

"He is speaking Galactic and is angry he did not know how much you mean to Etteria, to me."

"To you?" Her gaze met his. "I thought you hated me." She glanced away.

"Never, Ava." He stole a quick kiss. Lowering her to her feet, he was careful to ensure she remained covered, a challenging task when he fought the urge to rip the garment off her. He laced her fingers through his and pulled her against him.

"What do you mean she is his Dar Eth? I thought Dar Eths were extinct," Barro growled, and at his words, his mouth dropped open, at last realizing what Ava did mean to Etteria. "I asked for too little."

"You did, my yellow friend," Citus thumped Barro on his shoulder. "Do not be alarmed, Barro. I'll leave Etteria's navigation charts in your new scimitar."

"Truly?" Barro raised his unibrow on one side. The Etterians were ever-expanding their knowledge of the universe they occupied. To receive their charts would assist Maloid greatly, this Citus was more than aware of. It was a generous offer.

"And I suspect Xeus would want to thank you personally."

"Sweet talker." Barro rasped a laugh. "Lady Ava." He faced her and smiled. "Do believe you tempted me to keep you, angel," he hissed in Yithian.

She laughed, tugging free of Kanzo to wrap her arms around Barro's waist.

Kanzo grumbled, displeased at her open affection for any male other than himself.

"Thank you, Ambassador Barro. I will never forget your kindness." She stepped away to lace her fingers with Kanzo's again.

Kanzo nodded his thanks at the Ambassador and Prince Citus.

Citus said, "I will comm you the delivery location of your new ship. May Alllero shine upon you."

Relief settled on Kanzo as he escorted Ava through the front door. Citus finishing as per the Maloidian custom meant the agreement was final. Ava was Kanzo's uncontested by any Yithian or Maloidian. He glanced at her sweet face and laughed.

Chapter Fourteen

Etterian Scimitar, Eshima
En route to Mascroba, Yithia
The Communications Room

KANZO SCANNED THE MALES crowding them when they ported onto the scimitar. "Ava, this is the scimitar *Eshima*, and these males are her crew. This is Data Officer Kemt, who helped to find you."

"Thank you, all of you," she hissed in Yithian. When they frowned, she whispered, "Can't they understand me, Kanzo?"

"Not when you speak Yithian," he teased. Her eyes widened, and her mouth dropped open. She tempted him to kiss her again. "Try speaking in English, *thamani.*"

Thamani? She mouthed the word, arching a brow at him.

He grinned, excited to know how she'd react to what that endearment meant. But he would be patient. For now, he waited for her to try her English. She scrunched her nose and concentrated, but her adorable face twisted into despair when she couldn't switch. Fear darkened her tear-filled eyes. He drew her close to him and ran his thumbs across her cheeks, sweeping her tears aside.

"Do not worry, Ava, I am certain it will return." He addressed the males and instructed them to access the Yithian language protocol. "Now speak to them again."

"Thank you, all of you." Her smile stiffened.

He wanted her alone, to ask her what she was thinking. She tried to control her sadness, to suppress it, but humans were too expressive. Her eyes shimmered with fresh tears. Her tiny white teeth nibbled on her bottom lip, and her slumped shoulders made him want to gather her against him forever.

She faced Kemt. Reaching for his hand resting at his side, she gripped it in hers and shook it twice. Why only twice Kanzo didn't know. Michel shook three times, so there had to be a significance to the repetition.

"Thank you, Kemt."

Kemt cupped her hand with his and smiled. "At your service, milady."

Kanzo released a low grumble, not liking another male touching her. He wanted to rip their hands apart, to cover her body with his.

At his warning, Kemt's skin darkened, and he dropped her hand to return to his console. "As soon as we have ported the supreme commander and Prince Citus, we are to set course for the *Gladio*. They require assistance with the prisoners."

"Prisoners?" Kanzo frowned, sucking in deep breaths to calm his unexpected aggression.

"Supreme Commander Ulriq has located his human Dar Eth and awaits assistance. They have sought refuge in an abandoned mine and require porting."

"Dar Eth?" Ava asked Kemt.

He twitched, realizing they hadn't reverted to Galactic, not that they had anything to hide from her. This was more for him since he had yet to reveal the extent of their relationship.

"Is his Dar Eth Jack?" She raised her glistening and beautiful gaze to him.

He growled, and unable to resist, he descended to steal a kiss. "Yes," he breathed across her mouth.

She frowned. "Why's Jack on Yithia?"

"They stole her for the arena."

Ava winced. "I knew they took me by accident, but I hoped Jack had lucked out." Her smile was tremulous but no less joyful. "And your commander found her?" She laughed and flicked a dismissive hand. "You just said so. Dar Eth isn't a Yithian word. Did you say Citus is a prince? I can believe that."

"Two to port," Kemt said in general. Seconds later, Citus and Xan appeared before them. "We are en route to the *Gladio*, Supreme Commander."

"We are?" Xan scowled.

"Supreme Commander Ulriq has requested assistance. Stranded in a mine, twenty-two prisoners and his Dar Eth require extraction."

"Another?" Citus rubbed his palms together.

"The scimitar *Yakin* cannot handle that capacity," Kemt said.

Xan ran his gaze over Ava still in her revealing outfit. He flicked a glance at Kanzo who pulled her into the curve of his body, wishing he could cover her.

"Kanzo, see to your Dar Eth," Xan ordered.

"We dock with the *Gladio* in fifteen, Xan. Request accommodation for Ava as befitting her status." Citus's countermand darkened Xan's visage.

Kanzo hid a chuckle, burying his face in Ava's neck to do so.

"I do believe this is still my scimitar and my males," Xan said in a deathly soft voice, one Kanzo heard with his preternatural hearing.

"And you are still a pain in the ass, Xan," Citus slapped his battle-bond on the shoulder.

"Truly, Prince Citus, that honor is solely yours." Xan harumphed.

"I have also requested a medic be in-bay." Kemt tapped away at his multi-lit console.

Kanzo frowned at Kemt. He lowered his gaze to Ava. The medic was for her.

"A medic?" Xan and Citus echoed Kemt in unison.

The battleship *Gladio* loomed larger as Kemt sped toward the bay. He was coming in too hot, too fast. Kanzo nudged Ava into a seat and strapped her in. She raised her gaze to meet his, fear flashing across her features. He gritted his teeth, hating seeing that emotion.

"I need you safe." He tucked a curl behind her delicate ear.

The scimitar banked, swinging its tail in a whine of the usually-silent engines. He grabbed the support bar, his body bending away from her. Her hands shot out to grip his hips as if to keep him near, something he appreciated no matter the futility of her gesture.

"Damnit, Pilot," Citus growled, but Xan roared his joy, jumping up and down, his energy renewed. "You approve?"

"Yes, it keeps my males battle-ready."

The ship touched down on the bay floor, as gentle as a feather. Kanzo kneeled in front of Ava, grinning as he unstrapped her, focusing on the task to avoid staring at her exposed thighs and barely contained breasts.

"He did it for the adrenaline rush?" she asked in Yithian.

"You understand?" His gaze rose to meet her stunning green eyes wide in surprise.

She smiled and brushed her fingertips over his arched eyebrow. He loved the casual manner with which she touched him, as if she knew she had the right.

"Milady, I am Medic Brynr, please allow me to escort you to your quarters." An older male intruded, his posture stiff.

Ava glanced at Kanzo, not understanding the male in front of them.

"Not without me, Medic," Kanzo said in Galactic as he assisted her to her feet.

Brynr gawked at Kanzo's eyes then grinned at Ava, his expression changing from stern to pleased. "Of course." He left the shuttle, striding down the ramp and into the bay.

Ava trailed Kanzo, her hand gripped in his. She glanced around the warehouse-sized bay then froze, blinking at the open bay door. With a gasp, she pressed her body against his. The bay opened into the wide expanse of space. He wrapped an arm around her, tucking her body in the curve of his.

"The shield is active, *thamani*," he hissed. She nodded but the fear didn't release its grip on her just as she didn't loosen her hold on his hand. "May I carry you?" He gestured to her bare feet on the grated flooring.

"Like last time?" She winced.

He frowned, recalling how he had tossed her over his shoulder. "No, there is no need to keep one hand free to defend us. Here we are not in danger." Her mouth fell open, then she blushed. His Dar Eth was so expressive. "I did like your backside under my hand. It is incredibly soft." He kept his voice low despite its hoarseness.

Laughing at her silence, he scooped her into his arms and followed Brynr. He glanced down to find she had rested an arm across his shoulder and one hand above his heart. She must have sensed his gaze since she lifted hers to meet his and smiled.

As soon as they entered her temporary quarters, he spun her, pinning her to his chest, to brush his lips across her parted ones.

"I like it when you smile at me." He narrowed his gaze on her soft expression.

"If it gets me into these kinds of situations, I'll smile more often."

Medic Brynr gave a false cough, calling forth an answering chuckle from Ava. Kanzo let her slide down his body, hearing the hitch in her breathing as she encountered his ever-present arousal. She stepped back, her breathing ragged. He grinned at how easily he affected her.

"May I scan you, milady?" Brynr asked when she faced him.

"She speaks Yithian, Medic Brynr, this is the issue."

The medic frowned, tapped into his O.D.I., and addressed her again. "May I scan you, milady?"

"Do you need me seated or standing?" she asked.

"As you wish."

She remained still while the medic scanned her with his forearm. He paused at her ear. His scowl shot a dart of fear through Kanzo.

"They forced an interpreter in, doing damage from your middle ear to your inner ear. Do you feel any pain?" Brynr asked, without glancing up from his O.D.I.

"I did in the beginning. Whenever Operative Twyl spoke to me, the words pierced my skull."

"The scan revealed no current pain, but there is evidence of healed lacerations caused by the interpreter's effects on your ear." He glanced at Kanzo. "There was bleeding on the ear, and the power capacitor of the interpreter was too strong for her human brain." He scanned her ear with the med-gun pulled from a pocket in his military pants. "I have done all I can for now. I can only hope the swelling will reduce on its own. Unfortunately, milady, the Yithian language may have overwritten your natural one."

She trembled. "I'll never speak English again?" A tear slipped free. "How will I speak to my sisters?"

"Would an O.D.I. harm her, Medic Brynr?" Kanzo pulled her into his arms. She pressed her face to his chest, sliding her arms around his waist. That she sought him for comfort pleased him.

"The O.D.I. will be harmful until the swelling has healed. I will send my findings to Medic Der."

"Thank you, Medic Brynr." She tilted her head to meet the old medic's gaze.

"I apologize that it was not joyful news." He left them alone.

She buried her face against Kanzo's chest, her body curling into itself.

"Do not fear, Ava, all with an O.D.I. can communicate with you," Kanzo said.

She frowned. "What is an oh-dee-eye? Is it a procedure?"

He grinned, lifted his forearm, and activated his holographic buttons. "Optical Data Implant. It communicates with your neural system. It is how I communicate with you."

"I saw these on all your males." She rubbed her chin across his chest, burrowing into his arms. "Is Jack hurt like me?" She tugged out of his embrace to meet his gaze.

"No, she had an O.D.I. installed before they took her, so when the Yithians activated her language protocol, they unwittingly activated her tracker."

"But she's fine?"

"Yes. We will collect her and Ulriq soon," Kanzo said. Ava flashed him a bright smile and snuggled closer, releasing a contented sigh. "As much as I enjoy holding you, and believe me I do, perhaps you should cleanse and dress into something less..."

"Pornographic?" she whispered, not realizing it was an English word.

Kanzo's breath hitched at the use of her natural language but also at the meaning of the word his O.D.I. vividly explained. He wanted to push her, assist in the return to English for her benefit, but her brain was swollen, injured, and any assistance he offered might exacerbate it.

"You'll have to cut the skirt from me, Kanzo. Vlax made sure it wouldn't come off by accident...or ever." She broke away, yanking on the strips to prove it.

His gaze traveled over the sashes and frowned. She wore no undergarments beneath the fabric. And when he removed it, her naked beauty would be before him.

"What bothers you, *thamani*?" He needed to know her thoughts. Did seeing her so exposed worry her? Did she not trust him to do this for her without harming her? "I promise not to hurt you."

She gasped at his words and raised a tearful gaze to him. "I trust you, Kanzo. It's just that I haven't been naked in front of a man—"

Kanzo dusted his lips over hers. "I understand, Ava."

And he did. He needed to earn her trust and respect. Now that she was with him, he'd prove himself worthy of her. Dropping his arms from around her, he pulled a dagger out of his boot. With blade in hand, he stared at her hips, at the thick band from which the semi-transparent sashes hung.

"Where should I start?" he asked.

She glanced at the skirt then slipped a finger between her hip and the waistband. Her smallest finger squeezed through, but it was tight. It wasn't enough space to slide in a Maloidian dagger without harming her.

"If you could get your fingers in, you could tear it like you did my collar." She scowled then sucked in her stomach. "There. If I hold my breath, your knife might fit." She tapped below her belly button.

A shudder ripped through him, but he drew in a deep breath, prepared to do what she needed.

A brown dot on her right hip snared his gaze. He wanted to press his lips to it and trail a hot, wet kiss across her soft stomach. The sashes draped, slithered between her thighs, wrapped around her calf, distracting him. He lifted the front sash and sliced it off. He did the same to a few more until the front of her was bare, her femininity hidden behind black curls. The scent of her was rich and intoxicating. He fell to his knees and positioned trembling fingers above her curls. With a tight grip on his dagger, he pointed the sharp edge away from her skin.

"Inhale," he growled, his guttural voice beyond his control.

She drew in a deep breath, and he flicked the blade. The skirt pooled at her feet, on top of which he placed the dagger. He looped his arms around her backside and buried his face in her stomach, pressing an open-mouthed kiss there, tasting her skin as he'd longed to do. To truly have the taste of her on his tongue. He tightened his arms as he fought the urge to bury his nose in her curls.

"Kanzo?" She rested her hands on his shoulders but didn't push him away.

"Give me a moment, *thamani*," he said, his voice animalistic.

"What's wrong? Please... Please, talk to me." Her quavering voice meant he was frightening her.

"Do you remember when we met? How I fell to a knee?" He rubbed the tip of his nose across her stomach, not quite ready to release her.

"Yes, it looked like you were in pain." She stroked the hairs at the nape of his neck, making him shiver.

"I was. I still am." Shifting to the side, he kissed that brown dot, rumbling with contentment.

"What? Why?"

"It happens when an Etterian male meets the female who will become the center of his world." And he had yearned for it but had forsaken the dream. Yet here she was, in his arms, so warm and enticing.

"One of us is your female? Are we biologically compatible?"

"Yes, and yes."

She tapped his arms, and he grudgingly lowered his arms. Glancing at her, he was met with a glare, her green eyes bright with fury. He frowned, what had he said?

"You plan to test each of us to find out which female inflicted the pain?" She stumbled back and scooped up the discarded strips, holding them in front of her like a shield.

He scowled at her needing to hide from him.

"I do not need to test. Every cell in my body knows the female." He jumped from his knees to his feet, striding toward her. Startled, she shifted back until her bare backside hit the bulkhead. "And if this female will not cleanse and dress, I will take her nudity as an invitation."

Her mouth parted, and her eyes widened, only to warm with joy. She liked that she was his female.

"*Thamani*, please." He opened the cleansing door to usher her inside but paused. A strange black pattern on her left leg, from her hip to mid-thigh intrigued him. It swirled in an exotic design as intricate as Maloidian markings. "Ava, what is that?" His heartbeat spiked as hot need crashed through him. Why would the sight of such a marking fire his blood so?

"It's a tattoo." She twisted to show him her bare thigh. "It's Chantilly lace—"

"It is beautiful." He traced one detailed leaf with his fingertip.

"I saw it on a dress and thought it—" Her gasp preceded the tiny tremors racking her body as he caressed the intricate pattern. Bumps formed along her skin, trailing the shivers. He loved that she liked his touch.

"Is it permanent?" he asked in awe, his fingertips still stroking across the tattoo, feathering from hip to mid-thigh and up again. He was unable to cease touching her silky skin.

"Yes." She released a moan with her head falling back.

"Good." He rose to his feet, snatched a kiss, then shut the cleansing door on her.

Chapter Fifteen

Etterian Battleship, Gladio
En route to Battleship, Kushin
An Officer's Quarters

"I AM PLEASED YOU found a wrap, *thamani*." Kanzo smiled when she stepped out of the cleansing room. He tried not to stare. Even in the simple white garment, she took his breath away.

"I knew how to use a cleanser, thanks to my keeper, Vlax, right up to the blue button. That I learned only after my second cleanse." She chuckled before choosing a comfy and lifting her right knee to rest her chin on it. "I took a chance on the gray button."

His gaze darted between her exposed thigh to her eyes, to her expression, seeing no intentional enticement, no realization she tempted him.

"What do you want to wear?" He strode toward the replicator, activating it.

"You..." At her one word, his head shot up, and his lips parted. "...can choose for me, Kanzo." She had repositioned herself in her comfy, hence the delay between words.

Regardless of the why, her pause had made his malehood throb. He wanted her to wear only him. *Soon.*

"You would trust me with this?" He struggled to regulate his breathing, taking a moment to lower the temperature control in his suit. She didn't understand the significance of her trust. To defer to a male and allow him to clothe her was to publicly state her willingness to mate with him.

"Yes, you know what to expect in the next few hours. I could be shot at, tossed into a shuttle, stolen by another shark, meet a king..." She shrugged.

"Shark?" he whispered and waited for his O.D.I. to explain the English word she had unknowingly snuck into her speech. Once he saw the image, he grinned. His Dar Eth could be amusing.

"Be reunited with your sisters?" he said with a teasing smile. She grinned. Heat trailed where her gaze traveled over his form as if she caressed him with her soft palm. "Not if you look at me like that," he mumbled. "Come, enter in your sizes, then I will choose."

She jumped up and crossed to him to stare into the glass.

He altered the replicator's language to Yithian for her to understand the requirements. Within minutes, she was in the cleansing room, tugging on a pair of dark gray leggings and a pink floral tunic that sashed around her middle. He'd chosen garments similar to what she'd worn the day they'd met.

"Thank you, Kanzo. I feel almost human again." She twirled for him as she strode toward him still standing by the replicator. With care, he lifted her hair from the collar until it flowed down her back.

"My pleasure, *thamani*. Hungry? Thirsty? Come, choose something," he said. "I can see you are not well-nourished."

"I've lost a little weight, but you say that like it's a bad thing," she smiled.

"I need you healthy, Ava, to be by my side for a long time."

She glanced away to hide her surprise and the tears forming in her eyes

"What did I say, Ava?" He looped his arms around her waist, keeping her near.

"I didn't know you wanted me long-term. I'm sorry, but I haven't thought past today." She peered at him. "I don't mean to offend you by being honest. Although, the idea of spending more time with you makes me nervous and excited, like fireworks exploding in my stomach."

Fireworks? Yet another English word. He waited for his O.D.I. and the description puzzled him. Fireworks were small explosive pyrotechnics used for entertainment purposes. And this was happening inside her?

"Does it hurt?" He ran his hand over her abdomen.

"No." She laughed, the sound husky and alluring. "It means you affect me but in a good way."

"Oh. Then I too feel these fireworks. I like holding you. Every night, just before seeking sleep, I vowed to myself that when I found you, you would remain in my arms." He ran his fingers through the tangle of her hair. "Now, choose something to eat."

Sighing, she chose a square food called a sandwich and a small glass of exotic fruit juice. She offered him half her meal, and he grudgingly consumed it since she refused to finish it. Then she shared her juice with him.

He frowned. "You did not eat enough."

"Neither did you," she teased, but he remained displeased. "I lived off water for a few days, Kanzo, then on soup. If I eat too much now, it will make me sick." She patted his knee. "If it makes you happy, I'll eat small amounts often."

"That is acceptable. Thank you, Ava." He rose, laced his fingers with hers, urged her to her feet, and led her to the door. "The shuttle will be leaving for the *Kushin.*"

"And Jack?"

"Ulriq has reunited her with your sisters." He paused to read the transport status off his O.D.I.

"We are late? We missed her arrival on the *Gladio*?" She stomped her foot. "What now?"

"We prepped a shuttle for your departure. Jack traveled with Ulriq and Mich. We will leave when you want to, Ava." He brushed his fingers across her cheek, unable to stop himself from touching her.

"That is such a waste of resources." She huffed.

"You are a Dar Eth. There is nothing Etteria would not do for you."

"Dar Eth? Kanzo, what does that mean?"

"It means the center of my world, *thamani.*"

Her breath hitched at his words. "I am *your* Dar Eth?" Her luscious mouth dropped open again.

He frowned, his rush to reach the *Kushin* warred with his need to kiss her. He gave in and brushed his mouth over hers, but didn't deepen the kiss. "Yes, as Jack is Ulriq's Dar Eth," he said into her mouth, dazed at the small taste of her.

"And what would I call you if you were the center of my world?" She flashed him a teasing smile, allowing her hands to rest palms down on his chest.

"Eth," he said, his voice dropping an octave above a whisper.

She brushed her taut nipples across his chest as she slid her hand down to grab his hand.

"Come, my Eth, the *Kushin* awaits."

At her implication he was the center of her world, he growled. Dropping her hand, he looped his arm around her waist. He spun her to press her back against the bulkhead.

At her surprised gasp, he crushed his mouth to hers, delving in to taste her as he yearned to do. His tongue swirled around hers as he pinned his hard edges to her soft body. He moaned into her mouth, telling her how much he wanted this, how pleased he was to kiss her.

"Maker," he said into her mouth, allowing his reverent fingers to touch her, along her neck to her collarbone, to grab her upper arms. "I adore the taste of you." He opened his eyes to gaze into hers and moaned at the sight of her lustful expression as she licked the taste of him lingering on her lips. "Alodon's balls, what was I thinking?" He grumbled at his lack of control. With a deep breath, he laced his fingers through hers and left the quarters, pulling her behind him.

Chapter Sixteen

AVA TIGHTENED HER GRIP on Kanzo's hand when she stepped off the shuttle onto yet another bay floor, its massive doors gaping. A squeal pierced the mechanical din. Vicky ran toward her, the tears on her face called forth her own. Ava wrapped her arms around Vicky, squeezing her, but she didn't seem to mind. Ava flashed a watery smile at Taylor and Jack, who soon joined the hug, then the unmistakable smell of Michel followed. There was chattering and questions asked, not that Ava understood any of it. Too ecstatic to be back with her family, she didn't care at that moment. But when they paused waiting for her to speak, she stepped back into Kanzo's embrace.

"Please tell them," she said, grateful that he hadn't abandoned her to face this on her own. "Tell them I can't understand them."

"What the hell, babe?" Jack lisped, anger hardening her features. "What do you mean you can't understand English?"

"Sorry, Jacks. Damn shark injured me when he inserted the interpreter." That got another hug from Jack, tight enough to cut off her breathing.

"They do look like sharks, right?" Jack's laughter puffed warm air onto Ava's scalp. "Thought that was just me."

Arm in arm, they watched as Kanzo explained in a foreign language while showing Vicky and Taylor on his O.D.I. how to activate Yithian.

Vicky's head snapped up, and she lunged, bumping Jack out of the way with her hip. "Welcome back, Ava-honey," she said, giving her another quick hug. "I sound like a hissing cat."

"So, what happened?" Taylor asked from within Mich's arms.

"Oh, nothing out of the ordinary." Ava smiled, ignoring Kanzo's snort. "Until Kanzo rescued me, of course." She gave him a wink and blew him a kiss, replacing the smirk on his face with a lustful expression. That her ovaries reacted to his intense ice-blue eyes was for her knowledge only. "And you, Jacks?"

"A long, long story," Jack smiled. "It's why my O.D.I. was set to Yithian."

"Lady Ava, Warrior Kanzo, I am pleased to see you have returned safely," Citus greeted.

"Thank you so much for your assistance, my prince." Ava bobbed a curtsy, feeling awkward doing so.

"My prince?" He flashed a teasing smile. "You may address me as Citus."

Ava ducked her head. Calling a prince by his first name? What a strange culture. And when she'd curtsied, he'd blinked. She scanned the bay. No one paid him any attention. Maybe royalty didn't mean the same thing to Etterians.

"Will you be leaving soon, my prince?" Kanzo asked too formally as he tugged Ava away from Jack.

The prince barked out a laugh. "Yes, I will be leaving shortly, Warrior Kanzo. I have seen Vytus, my son, and am now determined to rush home to rub this in Xeus's face."

"This is not possible, my prince. Prince Enyl has also found his Dar Eth," Ulriq said as he strode toward them, then hooked his arm around Jack's waist and pulled her against him.

"Alodon's balls." The prince's disappointment was palpable

"His one to your two?" Ava said.

"Three," Vicky said.

"What?" Ava gasped.

Vicky gestured to the male watching her from the raised platform. She threw a sweet smile at him. Next to him, stood a young Etterian girl, who, Ava assumed, was his daughter.

"Mine, apparently." The blush staining Vicky's cheeks said it all.

Ava grinned, seeing how smitten her sister was.

"Thank you, miladies. I bid you farewell." Citus bounded away.

Ava's trailed him with her gaze then settled on another male walking toward them. She broke into a delighted smile when she recognized him.

"Welcome back, Kanzo," Danic said with an arm clasp and a shoulder grip. Kanzo grinned, as pleased to see him as Ava was. "Lady Ava," he said, taking her offered hand to give it a squeeze.

Kanzo's frown surprised her though. One moment he was happy then the next, his smile was gone.

"Danic, it's wonderful to see you," she said.

Kanzo scowled. He grumbled something under his breath but only received a grin from Danic for his trouble. Although, he did move away to greet the other females.

"Kanzo?" She faced him, wanting an explanation. What had Danic done?

"You are mine, *thamani*. With Danic near, something has a death grip on my chest. No male should look at you, should touch you." That he was jealous made her breath catch, then the full meaning of his words hit her.

"I can't have male friends?" she squeaked.

"Not Etterian males. You are enticing to all males without Dar Eths, especially your scent. To befriend them is cruel."

That was silly. How dare he forbid her. "But Nerx, Aaro, and Danic?"

"They are my battle-bonds and will endure your scent for my sake. I ask, Ava, that you show them kindness." At his request, her anger melted.

He was sweet to ask her to spare his friends as if she held such power over them. Wait, had he said her scent enticed his males?

"My scent? But I haven't used perfume since we left Earth."

He shook his head. "Fragrances are not preferred. It is too sharp and artificial. It offends our senses."

"Is that why there are no soaps or shampoos?"

"Yes, but our cleansers are set to clean all of your body," he said, his lustful expression returning. His gaze lingered on her hair, her face, her breasts, her thighs then he grumbled as if he disliked the direction his thoughts had taken him.

"So, if I wore perfume in their presence, it might mask my scent? Would that help?" At her offer, his gaze returned to hers, surprise warring with desire in the pale-blue depths.

"I am fighting the urge to throw you over my shoulder, to find a bed, and to appease the Ethera driving me."

Her breath hitched at his words. The need for him to do so gripped her, and she found herself stepping into his arms. He hugged her and placed a kiss on her temple.

"Ethera?" She splayed her hand over his chest, liking the velvety feel of the thick muscle beneath her fingertips, the heat permeating her skin, and his spicy cologne. Drawing in a deep breath, she was content to wait for his answer.

"The life force bond between Eth and Dar Eth. It is powerful enough to bring an Etterian male to his knees. Don't wear too much fragrance, *thamani*, we do not want to drive my battle-bonds away." His smile was teasing as he cupped her hand resting against his chest, trapping it there.

Chapter Seventeen

Etterian Battleship, Kushin
Traveling toward Earth.

"How is she truly?" Danic asked as he followed Kanzo into his warrior quarters. "We had to speak Yithian. I do have to admit, with their soft voices, the lisping is almost birdsong."

Kanzo explained the injury inflicted upon Ava and the lasting effects.

"Prince Citus and Supreme Commander Xan assisted in her rescue?" Danic tapped his fingers on his thigh.

"Yes," Kanzo said, reliving seeing her in chains, her revealing sashes parted by her muscled thighs, remembering where his mouth had been hours earlier. With a start, he realized Danic grinned at him. Kanzo drew in a deep breath and continued, "She was fortunate. A Yithian protected her, then the Maloidian Ambassador bought her from King Urio and sold her to Citus."

"Sold? Just how much does a Dar Eth cost?" Danic stopped tapping. "And where might I purchase one?"

"Twenty thousand tokens, a Scimitar, and an Etterian favor. Prince Citus would have doubled it had Barro realized her value."

"A Scimitar?" Danic gaped before flashing a smirk at Kanzo. "Ready to admit she is worth more? Worth your control? Your honor?"

"She is worth my life," Kanzo said with conviction. More than his life if he was honest. That she wasn't aware of this bothered him. He wanted her to know but feared her knowing. His indecision was uncharacteristic of him.

"Good." Danic huffed. "I was losing patience with your idiocy."

"You were not even there," Kanzo said, pointing out the obvious.

"True, but you know how I prefer quick victories." Danic chuckled. "Aaro and I are not long for *Kushin*. They have assigned us to the *Valiant*."

Kanzo's head shot up at this news. "When?"

"The shuttle departs within two days. The *Valiant* will escort the *Kushin* to Earth and remain there while you return home."

Kanzo scowled as he realized why Danic was telling him this. He didn't want to bid Ava farewell, he wanted Kanzo to do it for him. "Why is she fond of you, Danic?"

"Perhaps because I spoke to her on Earth. She is an amazing female, Kanzo."

"You were kind to her," Kanzo sighed, now understanding. He hadn't been welcoming toward her, and though the pain had been excruciating, it didn't excuse his behavior. He was an Etterian male with tested self-control, he should've handled his reaction better.

"Yes, I am fond of her, Kanzo but her scent is too..." Danic shuddered. "I would prefer you told her." Kanzo nodded, as he'd expected. "Der has informed me the Ethera is particularly overwhelming in your lineage."

Kanzo glanced at Danic, raising an eyebrow in query. "When did you learn this?"

"After you went berserk, destroying Der's medical. The annals recorded your ancestral father, Senzo, as finding it challenging,"

Kanzo scowled. "Why did I not know of this?" The knowledge would have been helpful, though to be fair, he hadn't expected to find his Dar Eth.

"You might have known had your blood-bonds still lived."

That made sense. He scowled at Danic. "I am in the annals now?"

"Of course. The annals record all pairings. Your ancestral father was one of the last traditional pairings to have occurred." Danic turned a comfy and dropped into it. "Now what is to happen? Ava is with the females and you are here alone?" He gestured to Kanzo's single unit.

"I do not know. I have yet to explain to Ava how the law addresses pairings."

"She does not know she is yours by law?" Danic shook his head. "Explain why she does not know this, Kanzo? Do you not want your Dar Eth?"

Kanzo scowled. "You say that as if I could reject her, Danic."

"She does not look as if she would reject you either. Although, when she mentioned Billy, this troubled me." Danic resumed tapping, this time on the underside of the comfy.

"What is a billy?"

"Alodon. She has not told you?" Danic closed his eyes. "It is a good thing I am for the *Valiant*."

"Told me what?" Kanzo asked, concern rising at the despair on his battle-bond's face.

"Ava almost mated a human male."

"Mated?" Kanzo repeated as he tensed at those words. His Dar Eth loved another male?

"Yes, they were weeks from mating when he died shortly after finding his pleasure in another female's arms."

"What male would not choose her?" Kanzo roared, clenching his fists at his sides. He was furious at this Billy, at Ava for not telling him, at himself for harming her. It explained why she'd believed he'd rejected her. Experience had taught her males would reject her and would choose any female above her. He suspected she believed herself the lesser among the human females, hadn't expected anyone to care enough to rescue her.

His arm buzzed, and he glared at the message. His eyes widened. Disbelief had him reading the words again. Within seconds, he was running, straight to Medic Der. Danic trailed but didn't pepper Kanzo with questions he couldn't answer.

"Are you certain?" Kanzo demanded of Der.

"Yes, if we do not remove it, they could track her or worse, send a kill signal."

"Alodon." Danic lunged across to a swaying Kanzo and punched him in the arm.

Kanzo glared at him, rubbing his bicep. "What did you do that for?"

"You looked like you might faint." Danic shrugged.

"Faint?" Der and Kanzo gaped. Etterian males did not *faint*.

Kanzo glowered at Danic for the suggestion of it.

"She needs you focused." Danic smirked, unrepentant.

"She does." Kanzo nodded, but he wasn't ready to admit he was grateful. "If you remove it, how does that affect the swelling or the language center of her brain?"

"I cannot say, Kanzo. Humans are an unknown species. I need to study their physiology. I could do irreparable harm, or she could return to her natural language. Pilot Ksal picked up the signal. Data Officer Prex verified it. It is weak but present."

"Can they not neutralize it without removal?" Kanzo wrung his hands, wanting to find the Yithian who harmed her.

Der shook his head. "Prex and I have analyzed all scans Brynr commed. It is not possible, Kanzo. We might disrupt other pulses or signals within her brain."

"I have to inform her." That strange death grip tightened Kanzo's chest again. "Where is she now?"

"In their shared quarters." Der messaged the information to him.

Kanzo read it off his O.D.I. and grunted. Two levels above. "How long does she have?"

Der shrugged. "I would prefer an immediate removal."

Kanzo broke into another run, not caring whether Danic followed or not since his upper arm still stung from the punch. But he had to admit, even to himself, he was in shock, and fear had gripped him. Fear was a new emotion for him, one he didn't like or know how to handle.

He requested entry, clutching the door frame while he awaited access. The moment it opened, he scanned those gathered until his gaze found hers.

Chapter Eighteen

Etterian Battleship, Kushin
Speeding toward Earth
The Girls' Shared Quarters

"So, what happened?" Jack lisped the moment she ushered Ava into her quarters. It was a replica of Mich's. Nerx had stipulated they could share or each receive their own, but the girls had opted to share or so Jack explained. "You look thinner. Did the sharks not feed you?"

"A white paste which was inedible, so I lived off water." Ava proceeded to tell them everything, even the mental letters she'd written.

"Wait, are you saying you're over Billy?" Vicky asked.

Ava laughed. "Billy who?"

"And forgave Kanzo?" Jack asked.

"Forgave?" Ava frowned. She hadn't realized she needed to forgive him.

"You looked super angry on the shuttle. I assumed he'd done something..." Vicky shrugged.

"Oh, that." Ava shook her head. She was such an idiot. "I thought he didn't like touching me, the way he tossed me over his shoulder like a bag of dirty laundry. He unknowingly defended this by saying he had to keep his fighting arm free. When I saw Prince Citus, at last, I had hope, and in abundance. Then when Kanzo entered the room..." She hummed, remembering seeing him jog toward her, his hands snapping her collar as if it was paper, the way he'd kissed her. She touched her lips as butterflies fluttered in her chest.

Taylor waved. "Whoa, jumping ahead here."

Ava blinked at her and blushed at their knowing looks. So, she told them about Vlax, his nickname for her, how he'd instructed her to please the king, and the meeting of said king. Her subsequent sale to the Maloidian Ambassador followed by her sale to Citus, and the way Kanzo had swept her off her feet. Who would've thought an alien man could be so romantic, so intense, and so damn handsome?

"And with you, Jack?" Ava faced her.

"Not much to say, kidnapped by an Etterian male named Teric, teleported to the Yithians, and found his daughter. They reunited us with Teric, we fought in the arena and killed two alien panthers, then Ulriq rescued me...us."

"And imagine, in such a short space of time, Jack's all aflame with longing for Ulriq," Vicky teased. "It took me ages to get her out of his tunic and into her own clothes."

"He smells so good." Jack dragged out the 'so' for emphasis.

"They do." Ava clapped. "Sun-drenched sheets, oranges, lemons, freshly cut grass and with no cologne."

"None?" Taylor gaped.

"Yes, it offends their senses." She settled her gaze on Jack. "Now what? What happens after they find their Dar Eths? It kind of sounds long-term."

Jack beamed. "It's forever, Ava."

"Forever?" She blinked.

The door chimed. Vicky hopped up to peer into the display vid next to the door then grinned at Ava. "It's Kanzo," she sang then activated the door.

The Etterian male stood there, filling the doorframe with his impressive, well, frame. Just seeing him made Ava's breath catch.

"Kanzo," she said, unable to smother a huge smile.

As his gaze met hers, his body tensed before he shuddered.

She hurried across to him. "What is it?" She ran her gaze over him, admiring everything about him right to the heavy-looking boots he wore.

"Please, Ava, you need to..."

"Sit." Danic gestured to the comfy, nudging Kanzo forward before entering the quarters himself.

"...hear this." Kanzo glared at Danic, before gathering her into his arms, holding her in that tender way of his. "The interpreter is..."

"It's a tracker? A bomb?" Her eyes widened. Now she understood his serious expression.

"How did you know?" He swept her hair off her temples. His shaking fingers alarmed her.

"I have an overactive imagination." She gaped, stunned at this news, and at how his body trembled. She pressed hers against his, needing him, needing his strength.

"Medic Der has requested an immediate removal."

Her shoulders slumped, having dreaded those words. "Kanzo?" She glanced at him, trying to hold back the tears. "Will you hold my hand?"

His breath hitched, and he crushed her to him, burying his face in her hair.

"Always." He pressed a kiss to her neck.

"What's going on?" Jack asked, rising from her comfy.

"Medic Der needs to see me." Ava attempted to shrug.

"Inform them, Ava," Kanzo whispered.

"They'll only worry," she said.

"I will inform them, you two go to Der." Danic held the door open.

"If you tell them, Danic, I'll be furious with you," Ava waved a finger in his face. At Danic's smirk, she realized the stupidity of her actions. Only a human woman would dare chastise an Etterian male. And she did dare.

"I told Kanzo about Billy, add that to my transgressions."

"I don't understand. Billy isn't a secret I needed you to keep." Ava faced Kanzo and rested her palm on his chest. "I didn't tell you, my Eth, because I don't think about him anymore. He is no longer in here." And she touched her chest, over her heart. The mental letters had helped free her. Somewhere between meeting Kanzo and traveling the galaxy, she'd let go of her grief.

"We will speak of this, *thamani*, I vow. For now, I need Der to ensure your good health."

"I know, to be by your side for a long time. I remember." She offered him a small smile. To have known him even for a day, was worth it. "I'm happy to have met you, Kanzo." She marched through the door, glancing at him over her shoulder since she didn't know the route.

He hesitated. "You are not leaving me, Ava. This is a simple procedure."

"Simple?" she said from the passage.

He strode toward her and gathered her hands in his.

"Yes, the device may receive a kill signal hence the urgency."

"It's not brain surgery?" she asked. When he chuckled, she wanted to hit him. "Are you laughing at me, Kanzo? You didn't tell me anything except that Der needs to remove it. For all I know, it's buried deep in my brain."

"I apologize for alarming you. The urgency is on my part, *thamani*. I cannot lose you again." And at his honesty, she gasped but hurried her steps, as well.

Chapter Nineteen

Kanzo raised their clasped hands for a kiss when Ava hesitated at the entrance of medical.

"Milady, I am Medic Der, thank you for coming so promptly," the medic hissed.

She squared her shoulders and tilted her chin, as if she prepared for battle. Kanzo couldn't fight the expanding heat in his chest. She was a remarkable female with a core of strength he admired.

"Kanzo assures me this is a simple procedure, Medic Der?" She crossed to the bed he stood next to.

Kanzo slid his hands under her arms and lifted her as if she were a *damu*. He lowered her to the bed, careful with the precious gift she was. A soft squeak had escaped her, and her hands had flown to grasp his shoulders. If Der hadn't crowded him, he might have stolen a kiss.

"It is, milady. I will send you to sleep to ensure you remain still for the removal." He lifted a med-gun and scanned her ear. "Your swelling has not reduced at all. I will take a few extra moments to ensure we speed recovery."

She frowned. "But it's only been a few hours since Medic Brynr scanned me, surely the swelling hasn't had enough time to reduce?"

"Our technology allows for fast healing. Your human biology is easy to mend. Some species are resistant to our med-guns and nano-meds."

"Thank you for explaining, Medic Der." She slipped her hand across the bed to grip Kanzo's.

His heart leaped into his throat, and he tightened his fingers around her more delicate hand, relishing her touch, liking that she sought his.

"Please lie down, milady."

"Only if you call me Ava, Medic Der. I'm not the daughter of a nobleman," she said before swinging her legs onto the bed without releasing Kanzo's hand.

Kanzo watched as she succumbed to sleep. Sighing, he released her right hand to move to the left side of the bed, slipping her left hand into his. He admired her, free to study her features with her mesmerizing eyes not drawing his attention. Her skin was paler than his but darker than Jack's. Her eyebrows and eyelashes were as black as his, and her tiny tilted nose was adorable. Her full lips parted in sleep, reminding him how much he liked the taste of her. Movement drew his attention, and he glanced up as Der inserted nano-meds into her ear. They would detach the interpreter, seeing it as a foreign object. He projected their progress onto his display vid as he tapped on his O.D.I., sending additional instructions as the nano-meds worked.

The robotic machines stripped the interpreter into pieces and transported them out. It was incredible to watch tiny inorganic pieces slip out of Ava's ear to rest on her cheek. They would not harm any part of her ear. Once this task was complete, Der instructed them to heal her swelling. In single file, they traveled deeper into her ear, along the main nerve, to the swelling at the top of her temporal lobe.

"The section of the brain that controls speech and language comprehension. It seems larger than it should be, but I can't be certain when her brain was the first of her kind I've seen," Der continued, sharing his thoughts with the procedure's recording.

The dark stain altered to match the surrounding brain tissue, but the size remained. When Der held a glass canister to her ear for the nano-meds to slide into, the procedure was complete.

"It was bruised but not swollen." Der capped the canister and stored the nano-meds in their temperature-controlled container. "The Yithian language has overwritten her natural one," he said glancing at Ava's face.

"She has spoken a few words in English," Kanzo said, stroking the soft skin of her inner wrist with his thumb. He couldn't stop himself from doing so.

"Perhaps there are no replacement words in Yithian?"

"That is correct. Shark was one of the words. None of our known worlds have such a creature." Kanzo's chuckle rumbled his chest.

"An apt word." Der grinned.

"How soon before you can install an O.D.I.?"

"Tomorrow," Der said before tapping the keys on his O.D.I. "She should awaken shortly."

"And the signal? I assume the dismantling of the interpreter disrupted it?" Kanzo took a moment to sweep a curl off her temple. An intense sensation gripped his heart—he didn't understand its meaning.

"Yes, the tracker, as well. I have amended my findings on such a device should we encounter any in the future."

"Is it out?" She rubbed her forehead then turned to smile at Kanzo. Her gratitude was easy to read. She'd expected him to break his vow until she realized he still held her hand.

"It is out,...Ava," Der said. "Any pain? Numbness?"

"I feel good." She grinned. "I hadn't realized I had a dull headache the whole time."

Kanzo squeezed her hand. Now to tell her the worst part. "Der is allowing the installation of an O.D.I. tomorrow if that would suit?"

Ava sat up in a single motion, implying she had strong abdominal muscles Kanzo was not aware of. His mind flashed to how soft her stomach had looked and felt on the *Gladio*. He tightened his grip on her hand.

"My English is gone?" she squeaked, instant tears forming in her eyes as she glanced between Kanzo and Der. Then with a firm nod to herself, she blinked the tears away and forced another smile, showing her inner strength. "Thank you for healing me, Der." She grabbed his hand to squeeze, before jumping off the bed, her other hand still in Kanzo's. "Come, my Eth. I'm pretty sure they're worried."

Chapter Twenty

Etterian Battleship, Kushin
Speeding toward Earth
The Girls' Shared Quarters

Her family took it well, understanding what had happened, the how and why she still spoke Yithian. They commiserated with her at the loss of her mother tongue, and through it all, Kanzo held her hand. Tears threatened to spill only once when Mich hugged her, whispering to her, as he had done through all those lonely years at the orphanage. *Everything will be all right, Angel.*

Regardless of their love and attention, she needed a few quiet moments to understand how she felt about it all, but being alone on a massive battleship wasn't an easy thing to achieve. She suspected that should she need to pee, they'd struggle to grant her that moment of solitude.

Kanzo holding her against his chest helped her fight her internal battle, to keep the impending breakdown at bay. She allowed her eyes to drift shut, to inhale his heated scent, feel the firmness of his muscled chest under her cheek, and indulge in the safety of his strong arms. When he stroked his fingers along her neck, she jerked awake, bumping her head on the bed beneath her.

"Kanzo?" she asked, alarm gripping her, fearing he was abandoning her.

"Sleep, *thamani*, I will see you in the morning." He kissed her temple and left her in the darkened room.

She flipped onto her side, enjoying lying there, listening to the voices coming from the main room. She couldn't hear what was being said. Only when she no longer heard male voices did she rise and stroll into the room.

"Ava, what's the matter?" Vicky bounded over.

She sighed. Like she had thought...no solitude allowed. She would have to take it, by force if necessary. "I...need to go for a walk, squirt."

"Do you think you should?" Jack stood next to the rehydrator with one hand on the glass.

"I miss running." Ava shrugged, starting to feel smothered, and angry that she had to get their permission to go anywhere.

"Be safe, and ask a male if you get lost." Vicky ushered her to the door.

Of all her sisters, Vicky understood her the best. Ava flashed a smile and ignored Jack's complaints. The moment the door shut, she hurried down a passage, taking random turns until she couldn't see any men, and the lighting had taken on a depressive tone.

She stood still and listened, trying to hear any sounds, voices, footsteps. When all she heard was a deafening silence, she crossed to the center of the passage and slid down the bulkhead to sit on the cold grated floor.

The tears fell then, unrestrained, and she let them. There was no one to see her here, no one to intrude. No one to think her reason for crying was silly. So, she'd lost her natural language? So what if her new language sounded like snakes hissing? She could still communicate, she could still laugh and love. But...when her thoughts stilled, a huge part of her foundation—the substance that defined who she was—was gone.

She didn't know for how long she cried. Judging by her swollen eyes and sniffling nose, it had been a while.

"Ava?" Kanzo whispered.

She glanced up in alarm, finding him on his haunches beside her. At the sight of him, she cried out, needing him, his touch, his scent, his presence.

"Kanzo." She threw her arms around him, sobbing anew, fresh tears splashing his chest. He dropped to the floor, pulled her onto his lap, and crushed her to him. Running his hand up and down her back, he whispered words in a lyrical language she wished she understood. As her tears dwindled, she sniffed and buried her face in his neck. Fresh heat stained her cheeks but wasn't hot enough to evaporate her tears.

"Do you want to know about Billy?" she whispered.

He tensed in reaction. "I recall Danic stating he had another female?" Kanzo growled. "He was a fool, *thamani*." He rubbed her back again. "It is good he died. I would kill him for his mistreatment of you."

She smiled. At one stage, she'd wanted to kill Billy herself. Fred had stated his willingness to resurrect Billy just to shoot him in the heart with the shotgun he kept behind the bar counter. "I was so ashamed. I was so blind, so easily deceived," she said in a small voice.

"You trusted him. You should not feel shame for doing so. He was the dishonorable one." Silence descended for a few minutes, and she moaned when Kanzo kissed her temple. "Did you love this male?" His voice was gruff with emotion, forcing her to consider his question and give him an honest answer.

"I thought I did," she said, "but when I look back, no, I didn't. I loved the idea of having someone to share in my life, who loved me."

Kanzo relaxed, but she didn't think anything of it. They were on an uncomfortable floor.

"Thank you for informing me, *thamani*."

Nuzzling his chest with her chin, she snuggled deeper into his embrace. "Kanzo? What language is '*thamani*?' What does it mean?"

"It is Etterian." He rubbed his jaw against the crown of her head. She waited for him to elaborate but he remained silent as if he didn't want to explain the meaning behind the word.

"It is beautiful." She leaned back to gaze at him. The dark made it safe to do so. He wouldn't see her tear-stained face, her red nose, her swollen eyes. She cupped his jaw and smiled. "You are a good man...male, Kanzo."

His breath hitched, and his heartbeat under her fingertips leaped.

"I do not feel like it some days, Ava." He hesitated before continuing, "I have not felt like myself for some time now."

"I know what you mean, like a part of you is missing."

He twisted to look at her making her think he could see her face. What an odd thing to do in the dark? "No matter how I *feel*, it should not change who I am." He emphasized the word feel as if it wasn't one Etterians used often.

"And who are you?" she asked, offering him another smile.

"I am an Etterian male," he said, arrogance and confidence embodied his words.

"An honorable one, Kanzo. Don't forget that."

"Not always, *thamani*," he said. "I am not as honorable as I need to be."

"That's nothing to be ashamed of either. Some days I can be unkind, rude, inconsiderate, judgmental, selfish, scared, anxious, sad...," she said. "Human women tend to be too emotional."

"Etterian males call it passionate."

Hearing the smile in his voice, she cuddled against his chest again, sliding her arms around his waist. "My point is, you can't be honorable all the time. It's impossible. I'm sure Ulriq's been dishonorable, even if it was just in his thoughts. I mean, Jack shook his world."

"Human females have that effect on the males they encounter." Kanzo's lips warmed her temple again. His fingers clenched her hip as if he needed her near.

She liked that, liked how the thought of it made her feel cherished. "We are a disruptive force."

"It is your softness we like." He squeezed her hip again, showing how soft she appeared to him.

"Softness? Like a pillow?" And here she'd always hated her hips. "How did you know where to find me?" So much for finding a quiet spot.

"Our males became concerned when they saw an unprotected female."

She winced. "So even here, I cannot be alone."

"You wish to be alone?" he asked in a wounded voice.

She grabbed onto his shoulders as if to stop him from leaving her. She hadn't meant to offend him or downplay how wonderful it was that he *had* found her. "Not anymore. I had a good cry. Thank you, Kanzo."

"I waited outside until I could not endure your pain any further," he said. She gaped. "We have excellent hearing."

"I'll remember that for next time." What else was supernatural about Etterians?

"If you wish to cry, then do as you normally would, Ava. I like you just the way you are."

His revelation warmed her. "You do? I thought I aroused you," she teased. Where she found the nerve to flirt with him, she didn't know. But the excitement gripping her chest made her carefree and...reckless.

"You do that too." He chuckled, teasing her in return.

She liked this side of him.

He rose to his feet, taking her with him in a smooth motion. Grasping her hand with his, he led her to a more populated floor, but it was better lit. With her free hand, she wiped at her face to reduce the effects of crying. Kanzo's stop was so abrupt, she slammed into his back.

"Now you are throwing yourself at me, Ava. What is a male to do?" he teased again, lifting his hands to her face to wipe her cheeks with the pads of his thumbs.

"What would you do?" She loved flirting with him. The charming smile summoning matching dimples made her heartbeat staccato. And that intense admiration in his eyes, admiring, had her feeling feminine and powerful.

"You *are* beautiful, Ava. There would be many things I would do to you and with you." He leveled his ice-blue gaze on her before grasping her hand.

As soon as they reached her quarters, she opened the door and turned to enter. But he stopped her with his long fingers circling her upper arm, above her elbow. With a tug, she fell backward, straight into his arms. He snatched a short kiss before giving her a gentle shove into her room. "I will find you later, *thamani.*"

Ava stared after him, resting her fingers against her tingling lips.

"That looked amazing," Jack said.

"It felt amazing." Ava smiled.

"Feeling better?" Vicky crossed to hug her. When Ava nodded, Vicky pulled her to a comfy and pushed her into it. "Good, meet Aala."

Ava settled her gaze on the young Etterian girl she'd seen when she'd first arrived. The poor thing twitched with nervousness and shyness tipped her chin to her chest. She toyed with the end of her braid, flicking it to the side and catching it. Big ice-blue eyes studied Ava.

"Hello, Aala, sweetheart. It's a pleasure to meet you," she said with the same tone she used when speaking to Lily. She held out her hand in greeting, which Aala happily accepted.

"Hello, Ava," she hissed-giggled.

"Has Vicky been treating you well?" Ava winked at Vicky who'd dropped into a comfy next to the girl.

"Of course, Jack too. Taylor is never here though. She and Mich are friends, yes?" The girl giggled, shooting Ava's brows up in alarm.

"I hope you won't mind, Aala, but I am desperate for a hug," Ava held her arms open, and Aala leaped across.

Ava chuckled and squeezed her gently. Aala soon slipped off to skip across to the rehydrator.

"What do you do all day? Is there a place to run on this huge thing?" Ava asked as she lifted her right knee to rest her chin on it. Sitting still for long kept restless energy pulsing through her.

"We found movies on the display vid, so that should make you happy. Also loads and loads of music." Jack hitched a thumb at the black screen mounted on the wall. "But other than that, they have an exercise section in the common. Though I doubt they will like it if you use it."

"Why not?" Ava asked.

"Ava? No male should look at you? Heard that yet?" Jack said.

"It's silly, I know. Like they can control where males look." Vicky huffed.

"It's because your scent is so good." Aala shrugged. "They cannot control males scenting their Dar Eths, so they try to control where they look."

"They need to trust more," Vicky said.

"They cannot, Vicky. Emotions are new to Eths, so are human females. If you were Etterian, you would feel what they feel, endure what they have to endure." Aala smiled. "But you are not Etterian and are therefore the unknown. They do not know how you feel toward them."

"How old are you?" Ava blinked, stunned at her maturity level.

"Twelve. In four years, I will need to attend The Gifting where I hope to find my Eth. But until then, I will live with Vicky and my father on Earth."

"Make sure Vicky introduces you to the other children. You may be a good influence on them." Ava winked at Aala but gave Vicky a pointed look.

Chapter Twenty-One

Etterian Battleship, Kushin
Speeding toward Earth
The Medical

"Are you ready, my Ava?" Kanzo asked as the door opened to her smiling at him in welcome. He stepped forward to hold her, relishing her softness against his body as he inhaled her scent deep into his lungs. He dusted his lips across hers and trembled.

"Yes, I'm ready for anything if you're with me." She laced her fingers through his.

Mesmerized by her upturned face, he jerked away and led her through the common to medical set up in one corner. As soon as she saw Der, she dropped his hand to approach the medic. The male smiled at her in welcome. She leaped onto a bed with her fingers pinching and releasing the fabric of her leggings—an indication of her nervousness.

"Medic Der, would now be all right for you to install this implant thing? I'm not bothering you, am I?"

Kanzo leaned against the bulkhead. How swiftly had his priorities changed. Only she mattered, her happiness, her wellbeing, nothing else, not even his honor.

"Never, milady.' Der smiled. "How are you this day?"

"Wonderful, so far. And if I remember correctly, I asked you to call me Ava." She lifted her gaze to meet his. "Is it a law to not use my name? Will using it cost you honor?" She gestured to Der's heel-length braid.

Kanzo liked that she knew this about his culture and considered it when dealing with their males.

"No, it is our way to honor you with a title."

"I'd appreciate it more if you learn my name, it implies you wish to know me, that I am valued."

"Very well, Ava. What is your handedness?" Der asked.

She gestured to her right hand, and he nudged her left, twisting it to expose her wrist. Kanzo watched closely, expecting Der to be gentle. Ava was softer than expected, and she needed a gentler touch, but he should not have worried. Der's touch was reverent.

"May I call you Der? I assume Medic is your designation?"

"You may call me Der, Ava," he said as he sprayed her wrist.

She shivered, and tiny bumps spread along her smooth skin. Then she looked away, squeezing her eyes shut to avoid watching what he was doing. A rumble began in Kanzo's chest, and he tamped it down. She behaved like a *damu* expecting pain. The urge to hold her had him in its grip. He folded his arms across his chest.

"It is done, Ava," Der said as he packed away his tools.

"What?" She gaped at her wrist, caressing the smooth skin of her wrist. No scar remained. "Are you sure? I didn't feel a thing. I didn't see anything either." See anything? With her eyes shut? She was so adorable, Kanzo's breath hitched, and he took a step, eager to sweep her into his arms.

Instead of taking offense at her doubting his skill, Der chuckled. "I am sure." He tapped her wrist twice. A holographic screen appeared with the standard options.

She gasped. Her right hand trembled when she raised it to touch a key. "How...how do I use it?" She looked at Der with awe and expectation.

He punched a message into his own O.D.I.

She squealed, her laughter breathtaking, drawing the attention of the males in the common.

Kanzo couldn't hold back an answering smile and relished the heat coursing through his body at her happiness.

"It tickles, Der." She showed Der her forearm. "Now what do I do?" He tapped her wrist again, and his message appeared. She read it then grinned at him. "How do I learn...Galactic?"

Der navigated to the Language Protocol section on her O.D.I. and chose the Galactic Language Protocol.

"Tell me, milady, what is an Algri?" Der asked in Galactic.

"They are six-eyed green aliens with twelve tentacles and are an unemotional species." Ava gaped, the pink of her mouth too tempting. Kanzo grumbled. "How did I know that?"

"The O.D.I. translates my Galactic into Yithian for you to understand. It has access to our data annals which it inserts into your mind. Like recalling a memory."

"Do you know how awesome that is, Der?" Ava squeezed his hand as she bounced on her toes.

"I assume it is this *awesome* by your reaction, Ava."

Her smile was sweet, startling the older Etterian male. Kanzo laughed at the sight of Der speechless. A rare occurrence, indeed.

"Now, the true reason why I need this, Der. Show me how to speak English…"

He selected the English Language Protocol, and with a glance at Kanzo, he stepped away from her.

"Do you understand me, Ava?" Kanzo asked in English and waited for her reaction.

She bit her lip. Tears welled in her eyes and overflowed as she nodded. If it wasn't for the wide smile on her face, he'd believe she was unhappy again. A cold hand had, for a moment, gripped his heart.

"I understand you," she said in English before squealing her happiness.

She bounced across to Der and hugged him, startling the poor male. Then she threw herself into Kanzo's arms, trusting that he would catch her. And he would, every time. She cried into his neck, a thousand tears, her arms crushing him. If this was her reaction to joyful things, he would endeavor to please her more often.

Chapter Twenty-Two

Etterian Battleship, Kushin
Speeding toward Earth
The Girls' Shared Quarters

"Are you alone? May I come see you, Ava?" Kanzo's image on the display vid was crisp and large. She sighed, admiring his square jaw and his fuller bottom lip with those ice-blue downturned eyes.

"This sounds serious."

"I have news, *thamani*, about Danic." In the way he said it, it must be bad. He seemed so distressed. She needed to be there for him as he had supported her.

"Danic? I'll wait by the door." She ended the connection, rushed to the rehydrator, and ordered a soda before crossing to the door. A few minutes later, the door chimed, and she commanded it to open. The sight of Kanzo in front of her, so tall, his attraction devastating to her senses, caught her breath. She wanted to hold his hand, wanted him to press kisses to her forehead, to brush those lips over hers, and God willing, kiss her thoroughly.

A pulse ticked at his jaw as his nostrils flared. He paled, but he stepped into the room, accepting the soda she offered him. His hand trembled. What had happened to affect someone of Kanzo's stature? He took a sip of the cherry soda before gesturing to her to assume a comfy. As soon as she did, he slid into the one next to her and placed his can on the table. He laced her fingers with his, tugging her hand up to his mouth for a kiss.

"What is it, Kanzo, what about Danic?"

"Danic and Aaro are on the battleship *Valiant's* roster, en route to Earth." His gaze traveled her face, as if he expected her to react in a negative way. She'd miss speaking to Danic, but it wouldn't be as devastating as Kanzo leaving.

"And you too?" Her mouth fell open in dismay. Panic cinched her heart, and she tightened her grip on his hand. She couldn't lose him.

"No, I will remain by your side. My primary task is to ensure your safety."

Her relief was short-lived. Her safety? She loved that he protected her, but they were on a battleship, why did he need to protect her? And above that, she didn't want to be an obligation to anyone. Instead of feeling gratitude, his words pulsed heat along her veins.

"I don't need a babysitter, Kanzo," she snapped, releasing his hand as if it burned her. His eyelids fluttered then he scowled at her. "Before we continue this fascinating discussion, what just happened? Your eyelids trembled."

He drew in a deep breath then released it. "When you use a word I am not familiar with, the O.D.I. informs me of its meaning."

She smiled at him, her thanks for explaining.

"I am not this babysitter. It is an honor to protect you, *thamani*," he said, and the sweetness of it surprised and charmed her. "Every male here would die to protect you."

And angered her again. She leaped to her feet, needing to pace lest she punched him. Like she was incapable of surviving on her own? Damn, but these Etterian men were arrogant, stubborn, treating women like they were children.

"That makes no sense, Kanzo. Your lives are as valuable as my own."

"You are precious to Etteria, to me, you know this. You make our lives worth living."

Then he said something sweet again. She blinked. "I assume they'll be gone for a while?" she asked, desperate to steer the conversation away from something that made her nervous and excited. *He said that she was precious to him. He kept on saying that, proving it with every gesture.* Her chest filled with butterflies at the thought. Since he'd rescued her, he'd shown his sense of humor, that he was honorable, caring, and sincere in his desire to know her. She wanted to get to know him, as well.

"Yes. What was your daily schedule? On Earth?" At his curiosity, she paced again.

"I used to run every day."

"Run?" He frowned.

"Yes." Excitement burst through her, that same feeling she'd had when she left home to enjoy her daily run.

"Just run?" His confusion echoed Vicky and Taylor's.

She couldn't help but grin. "I would like to see how you train, Kanzo. You look stunned, almost horrified. With humans, for most of our activities, running forms part of it."

"You just run, for no reason?"

She laughed taking pity on him. "You are welcome to run with me," she said, eager to share this with him. "We would have to get you a pair of running shoes, though. And find a place on this battleship to run."

"I accept." Kanzo rubbed his palms along her thighs. "May we replicate the footwear now?"

Her eyebrows shot up. Just like that? "You're not going to argue with me?"

"No, I trust you." His simple statement made her heart pound.

He trusted her, trusted that she knew what was best in this situation, no questions asked, no doubting her skill. Her breath hitched at this unexpected leap of faith, this gift he'd given her.

"And after this run, what do you do?"

"On this battleship? Breakfast then nothing, for the whole day." Her frustration was evident in her voice. Her shoulders slumped and a frown replaced her previous smile. "I'd suffer from boredom if I didn't have you to speak to. Vicky's with Aala, Jack's…busy, and I hardly see Taylor, as if Mich is trying to make up for lost time."

"And boredom is bad?" He arched an eyebrow.

"Yes. At home, I was always busy."

"What did you do at home?" He scooped up his can and wrapped his long fingers around the soda, dwarfing it. She shivered at the sight of those fingers, wondering how they would feel if they caressed her skin. "Ava?" he said, calling her back to the present.

She met his mesmerizing ice-blue gaze. He wanted to know more about her life on Earth.

But she was nervous about telling him. Judging by the length of their hair, cutting it for a living might not be acceptable, might even be against their religion. She chewed on her lip, deciding whether she should tell him or not. He waited for her to speak. He didn't try to convince her to tell him, just waited as if he had nowhere else he wanted to be.

"I was a hairstylist," she said, before drawing in a deep breath. "I cut hair." His eyes widened in shock, and she winced, expecting his horror to follow.

"That is incredible, Ava."

"It is?" she squeaked.

"It is a task most do not learn, and it falls to Adviser Cales to perform." He placed his now empty can on the table and swung his braid around, catching the tail. "When it grows too long, we trim it with a sharp knife."

Horrified at hearing this, she took his braid from his hand, to brush the soft ends across her palm. A few strands curled around her fingers. "On Earth, hairstyling is for vanity, but on Etteria, your hair is a mark of honor. Vlax taught me this."

"Many human females ask you to cut their hair?"

"Yes," she said. "And males."

"I understand. And would they not still require this skill on Etteria?"

Her brows shot up. Why, oh why, hadn't she thought of that? She could open Etteria's first hair salon. She gasped. The first interstellar hair salon. She gifted Kanzo with her widest smile.

"Would it be possible to send someone to Earth to collect my...tools?" In her excitement, she grabbed his forearm with both hands, dropping his braid in the process.

"Of course, Operations Commander Malo is serving as Ambassador to Earth. But would the replicator not assist, and if not, we have engineers who may construct whatever you need. We could also collect the tools when we deliver Vicky to her home."

"Yes, of course." Ava laughed, the sound bubbling out of her. "Would I have to ask your king for permission?"

"I could speak to him on your behalf."

Her mouth fell open at his offer. "You would do that for me?"

"Yes." His gaze met hers with an intensity she found breathtaking. "Did you run this morning?"

"No, I haven't found a place to run yet. It has to be a long uninterrupted path. When would you like to sort out your clothing?"

He smiled. "Now it is clothing?"

"Don't you have specific clothing you wear when training?" She arched a brow when he shook his head. "Humans do, and you want to be comfortable when you run."

He flashed a grin, dimpling his cheeks. Ava blinked at him, a little dazzled. She glanced away, drawing in a deep breath to steady her nerves.

"Let's sort out your clothing, specifically the shoes. They are the most important. Your quarters or will here do?"

"Here will do," he said with a gruff voice. His beautiful eyes dropped to half-mast.

She blushed with the realization his thoughts were sexual. Leaping off the comfy instead of lunging for him, she approached the replicator as if it could save her from his heated intensity. He went with her, crowding her to see the replicator's selections. Within minutes, she ushered him into the cleansing room to try on loose shorts and a running vest.

"I am attired for sleep." He stepped through the door.

She drooled. The vest was amazing on his muscled chest, revealing his incredible arms and his narrow waist. And the shorts brushed his knees. Her gaze riveted on his amazing calves. She'd never seen anything quite so beautiful on a man before. He had huge feet, now bare, and she blushed at the sight of them, wondering if the adage was true.

"It is comfortable."

"Good, now shoes." She cleared her throat, turning her flushed face to the replicator.

The sneakers took a while longer to select. She wanted him comfortable, needing him to understand why she enjoyed running so much. Not that she understood her desire to share this with him. She offered the replicated shoes to him, but he stood there staring at them, uncertain as to how to put them on.

"Sit, I'll help you."

He dropped into a comfy, and she grinned, kneeling to lift his foot onto her thigh. She peeled a sock on first before taking a shoe out of his hand. She undid the laces in slow motion so that he could see. Then, she slid it onto his foot and tied the laces into a bow. She gestured to him to do the same for his other foot, and he did, with determination. The concentration on his face, as he learned how to tie his shoe, was adorable. Standing up, she offered him a hand to assist him to his feet. He accepted and rose, but didn't release her hand. Instead, he tightened his hold.

"How does it feel?"

He blinked at her. "They feel comfortable," he said with a note of surprise. He stamped his feet as she demonstrated.

"Do you feel them pinching your toes?" she asked but he didn't reply.

He stared at her with a strange yet intense expression on his face. "I never wanted a Dar Eth," he said, his words startling her. "But you are intoxicating." He met her gaze, forcing her to keep eye contact when she wanted to hide her flushed face. "You fascinate me. Your beautiful green eyes, your facial expressions, the shape of your mouth."

Silence descended, and Ava struggled, not knowing how to respond to his declaration.

"Kanzo? The shoes?" she asked.

His open admiration had butterflies exploding in her stomach then he stroked a fingertip along her jaw to her earlobe. Their wings bombarded her insides, snatching her ability to breathe.

"My feet feel good." His voice rasped across her senses.

She clapped her hands, not having to pretend her delight. That he would try this with her meant so much. Billy hadn't liked exercise other than the horizontal kind.

"You are now ready to go running with me." She gestured to all of him.

He grumbled something under his breath and stepped away from her. His posture changed as if he was defensive.

She raised an eyebrow at him. "What has you so grumpy?" She had to ask when it was so easy to misunderstand between humans. An alien species dealing with human women guaranteed confusion. "You don't have to run with me, Kanzo. Please don't feel obligated. I'd hate that."

"I want to," he said too forcefully, as if he needed her to believe him.

"Then what's wrong?"

He captured her face between his palms, his touch gentle even as he trapped her. "I enjoy...spending time with you, Ava."

Her mouth fell open at his second revelation before breaking into a smile. "And grumpy is your automatic reaction to spending time with me?" She shook her head as laughter bubbled out of her. "Are you this grumpy in all aspects of your life, Kanzo? Even when you orgasm?" At his frown, she laughed again. She could just imagine him scowling mid-thrust.

"What is this orgasm?" He blinked in all innocence.

Her laughter fizzled, her eyes going wide in surprise. She hadn't considered an Etterian's sexual act was different from humans. "You know? When a man and a woman..." The tips of her ears burned, but when she glanced at him, his shoulders were shaking with silent laughter.

"I jest, *thamani*. No, I am not grumpy when I find fulfillment." He chuckled.

"Kanzo." She whacked him in the upper arm, hurting her fingers more than she could harm him. "I can't believe you teased me."

"I have never seen your face so dark." He grinned.

"Great," she said, not liking she'd blushed herself into ugliness.

"You look adorable," he said with huskiness. She snorted, despite his sexy voice making her stomach flutter. "I adore your eyes. They make me want to—"

Her gaze flew to his face in alarm when he stopped speaking. He trembled with his eyes closed and released her, clenching his fists hard enough to whiten them.

"Kanzo?" she squeaked and hurriedly cleared her throat. "Should I comm Der?"

"Give me a moment." His voice was octave above gravel. He sounded a little animal-istic.

"Are you in pain?" She raised her hands, wanting to comfort him but was too scared to touch him.

"Yes, I need you, Ava. I must hold out for a few more days," he said more to himself, drawing in deep shuddering breaths. "I cannot lose control." He squeezed his eyes tight as he bit down on his bottom lip.

"What happens when you do?"

"To lose control is unacceptable to warriors, Ava, and around you, I struggle to main-tain it. It is dishonorable for a warrior to feel, to fail."

"What?" She gripped his shoulders. "I threaten your control, your honor?" She pulled out of his arms and stepped away from him, trying to put some distance between them.

"With you, my honor does not matter."

She curled her shoulders to ward off a total meltdown. To the Etterians, honor meant everything, their lives, their social structure, their discipline, their hair. He must resent her. And she couldn't bear the thought that sweet, sexy Kanzo would come to hate her.

"I understand if you never want to see me again." She wrapped her arms around her waist, curling into herself as if doing so protected her heart. The idea of not seeing him ripped through her, snatching her breath as fear gripped her, crushing her heart. But it was preferable to him hating her.

"You are punishing me now, *thamani*," he said.

"I am saving you." She raised pleading eyes to him. Did he not see what she was trying to do? "I'm trying to help you."

"I need your touch, yours alone. You are my Dar Eth, only your touch will save me."

That would make an awesome pickup line if he was trying to get into her pants, but he wasn't. He had to sacrifice who he was and what he stood for. "Pain with honor or no pain with no honor? What kind of choice is that?" She wiped away a solitary tear, lest it encouraged all her tears to fall.

"A female must test a warrior's control."

"She must?" She scowled. What nonsense was this?

"Yes, to not lose control would worry our males..."

She pinched the bridge of her nose, fighting the unshed tears burning her sinuses and trying to make sense of this. "Your culture is confusing, Kanzo." She dropped her hand and faced him. "I don't want you to resent me, come to hate me... I couldn't bear that."

"I cannot hate you, Ava. As my Dar Eth, it is physically impossible for me to hate you." He opened his arms wide inviting her back. "Please, *thamani*."

She stepped into his embrace without hesitation needing his strength, his scent more than she cared to admit, even to herself. His sigh was deep when he wrapped his arms around her. She didn't know how long they stood there. He rubbed her back. She loved when he did that.

The display vid chimed, and she grumbled something under her breath before pulling out of his arms. He kissed her temple and disappeared into the cleansing room. The display vid chimed again, but she blinked, staring at the shut bathroom door. Just as she raised her hand to accept the request from Ulriq, Vicky entered the quarters with Aala in tow.

"Afternoon," Vicky said as she strode toward the rehydrator.

"Afternoon." Ava grinned and opened her arms for a hug from Aala. "How are you, my girl?"

"I am well, Ava. Greetings, Warrior Kanzo."

Kanzo emerged from the cleansing room, once more in his uniform, with his new clothes bundled under his arm.

"Good day, *damu*." He smiled and dumped the clothes on the nearest comfy.

But when Aala hugged his legs, his eyebrows shot up. He dropped to his knee to return the hug as gently as possible while meeting Ava's gaze over Aala's head. She grinned then answered the communication request.

Chapter Twenty-Three

Etterian Battleship, Kushin
Speeding toward Earth
The Common

"Jack, what the hell? You disappeared in the middle of the night. I hope he was worth it?" Ava said as soon as Jack's face appeared before her on the vid.

Vicky muttered something in the background then crossed toward Ava with a coffee in hand.

"So far, yes." Jack blushed.

Ava laughed at the sight of it, delighted to see her sister so happy. "Good. I want details later when Teric isn't eavesdropping." She'd caught part of his face from where he sat on a comfy.

"I am doing no such thing," Teric stepped fully into view.

Ava gave him a knowing grin.

"Hello, big guy," Vicky rasped.

"Greetings, *minus susa*." At the gruffness of Teric's voice, Ava shot a surprised glance at Vicky. Holy shit, that happened fast. Her smile morphed into a wide grin. Make that two happy sisters. Three if she counted Taylor.

"Father, look at my hair. Vicky did it. Is it not beautiful?" Aala stroked her French braid. Gone was her usual fish-tail braid, like Kanzo's.

Ava snuck a peek and flushed, finding his focus fixed on her.

"Everything is beautiful on you, *ensa*." Teric's unmistakable love for Aala warmed Ava's heart.

"Shall we meet in the common for lunch?" Jack asked. "I have a craving for a burger."

"Add fries and I'm there. With a strawberry milkshake?" Vicky said, excitement spiking her voice. "Aala, wait until you try one of those."

"We're on our way." Jack ended the communication.

"More Earth food?" Kanzo teased as he grasped Ava's hand in his, tugging her closer to him. As they trailed everyone, he squeezed her hip or stroked her neck, but didn't release her hand.

As soon as they entered the common, Jack rushed over to Ava. "May I borrow her for a minute, Kanzo?"

"Yes." He squeezed Ava's hand before letting go. "I will await you here, *thamani*."

With a sigh, she followed Jack to the viewing deck.

"I just found out I'm married." Jack offered her back to the high windows looking out into outer space.

"What?" Ava squeaked.

"Do you know anything about the Ethera?"

Ava frowned. "Not much. It's some sort of bond?"

"As Teric explained, when an Etterian male finds his Dar Eth, his soulmate, he experiences the Ethera. It calls forth strong emotions long suppressed. By the time a male might experience his Ethera, it releases all previous emotions in one occurrence, hence the pain-pleasure that drives them to their knees."

"Dar Eth is a soulmate?" Ava gasped. "I mean, Kanzo said I was the center of his world. I thought it was a pick-up line."

"It doesn't stop there, babe. When Ulriq experienced the Ethera, his commitment to me was instant. At that moment, he became my husband by Etterian law."

"No." Ava cupped her mouth. "Just like that?" Shock and envy warred within her. To have the decision taken out of her hands? Bliss. But did that mean she was married too as Kanzo's Dar Eth?

"Pretty much."

"And we don't have a say?" If there was leeway to annul the marriage, then the decision on the direction her life would take remained with her.

"I don't want a say. I want him, anyway I can get him. Ava-babe, we complain that men aren't willing to commit, but we can't handle it when they are. Kanzo's eager too."

Ava wrung her hands, then succumbed and paced. "I'm married? You're sure? I mean, he said I'm his Dar Eth, but we haven't discussed all the details."

"Yes, you're married. I expected this to upset you." Jack flashed her a grin. "This is me, babe, you can't fool me."

"No, I'm not upset, after all, they are aliens. We know as much about them as they do about us. It's just that he didn't tell me, Jacks. What kind of marriage will we have if it's not based on honesty and trust?"

"Well, they can't lie, so that's sorted."

"Neglecting to tell me is also a lie." Ava scowled.

"Not in his eyes. That you don't know doesn't occur to him. This is all common knowledge to them. Push him and see what he has to say."

Ava huffed at Jack who marched out of the viewing deck. She trailed in a dazed state, deep in thought as she considered this change in her life. As soon as they entered the common, Jack strode toward Ulriq who welcomed her into his arms with an unguarded expression on his face. Ava's heart ached at the love in his eyes.

Kanzo was her Eth. He told her that much, had said she was precious to him, that she was the center of his world. He'd followed his words with actions, keeping her safe, caring for her, wiping away her tears. What more could she ask for in a husband? And he was the only male that roused any sort of emotional response within her since Billy died. Her breath hitched with delight that it *was* him, nervous at this turn of events, and furious that he hadn't told her. But before she stripped him a new one, she'd do as Jack suggested and grill him on it.

"Ava? Are you unwell?" he asked as he jogged toward her.

Her breath came out in a whoosh, now seeing his attention for what it was. "Kanzo, I wanted to ask you. When we met and the Ethera drove you to your knee, you said it was painful?"

He grimaced. "It was unbearable. That was why I could not endure your touch, your scent. You still make me tremble, *thamani*, just being this near to you." His words tore through her.

She shivered under the influx of emotions claiming her heart. "You said I'm your Dar Eth. What does that mean? How does this change my life?"

"It means you are mine as I am yours."

She sighed, as beautiful as those words were, talking to him was like drawing blood from a stone. "So, if I decide to remain on Earth?" She tried another angle.

"I would remain with you, wherever you go."

"And if I fall in love with a man on Earth and I decide to marry him?" She restrained the wince at her question, unable to imagine a life without him. Scowling at her thoughts, she set them aside for now. She needed to analyze what she felt for the big Etterian.

"Love another male? Marry him?" He gaped. His eyelids fluttered, and he turned a ferocious scowl on her. "You cannot, you have *married* me." His voice hardened. His fingers curled around her upper arms as if to shake her. His touch was gentle though as if he couldn't bear to hurt her.

She almost smirked. At last. "I am? When and how did that happen?"

"Etterian law recognizes the Ethera as the final word, confirming the pairing under Etteria's protection. All males must prioritize the pair's safety."

"So, you married me on Earth?" She paused, waiting for him to nod before continuing. "For humans, you must ask me to marry you, Kanzo. I have to accept your proposal. You can't just marry me without my knowledge."

"You don't want me?" His expression showed his devastation.

Ice lambasted her face. She panicked. This wasn't how she'd foreseen this discussion going. "Of course I want you. But we're talking about you keeping something important from me. Jack said you assumed I'd know about the Ethera and how it impacted me. Why didn't you tell me about your law, Kanzo? Are you ashamed of me?" A vise-like grip squeezed her chest.

Ah, the heart of the matter, and she did feel this way. The panic must have cut through her mixed-up emotions. Why hadn't he claimed her as Ulriq had Jack? There was nothing wrong with Kanzo. He was perfect. The fault must lie with her.

"I am not ashamed of you, Ava." He drew her into his warm embrace but still maintained eye contact. His eyes burned with intensity, as if he begged her to believe him.

"Then it's you who doesn't want me?" she asked in a small voice. He was stuck with her, with a Dar Eth he'd never wanted. "Like Billy didn't want me?"

Kanzo crushed her to him, lifting her off the floor, to his height, just to bury his face in her neck. "I want you, Ava, I need you."

"Why? After all, we haven't known each other long, Kanzo. Not enough time has passed for us to have formed an emotional attachment."

"Why?" He echoed her question, disbelief in his voice. "Etterians do not need time. It is immediate. The moment we met, I knew you were mine. It is in me, Ava, to protect you, to care for you, above all things. To fight the Ethera is to fight myself, my nature."

"So, you're trapped?" Her breath hitched on a sob as pain lanced through her. Oh, how right her thoughts were, and it hurt being a know-it-all. Leaving Jack and her family to live alone would hurt too, but what other choice did she have?

"Trapped? I am not. The Ethera chooses for me better than I would choose for myself. And you are perfect to me, *thamani*."

Kanzo thought her perfect? She was desperate to believe him but still, a tiny sliver in her mind whispered dire warnings. "Then why am I not with you like Jack is with Ulriq, Kanzo?" She curled her arms around his neck, nuzzling her cheek across his temple.

"With all that has happened, I did not know how to proceed," he said, admitting his ignorance. "Whether we could... I could..." His arms convulsed around her, telling her how deep his emotions ran.

The idea of seeing him every day, waking up beside him, sharing showers and a bed, swept a wave of delicious warmth through her. Yes, she was happy to be married to him.

"And if you could, what would you do right now?"

His breath hitched at her question, and he shuddered beneath her touch. "I would adore every inch of you." His kiss on her neck was hot and demanding. His lips at her throat made her spasm with desire.

Ava liked the sound of that. "When, Kanzo? Where?" She pressed kisses along his jaw.

He jerked back to meet her gaze, startled by her surrender. "I live in the barracks. It is not acceptable to take a female there."

She frowned. She was, at last, able to have him but with no place to do so. "Then when we drop Vicky off? The quarters will be mine alone."

He gave her such a beautiful smile, revealing both dimples, that her breath caught. If she listened with care, she could hear her ovaries applauding at her brilliant suggestion.

"Put me down, Kanzo. If you keep holding me like this, any corner will do."

Scowling, he lowered her to the floor, allowing her to feel every hard edge of his body. She laced her fingers with his and pulled him after her.

They were in time to hear Ulriq's question. "What is a hot chocolate?"

"Were you listening in on mine and Teric's conversation?" Jack asked, shock twisting her face.

"I do not trust Teric," Ulriq said, his unrepentance not boding well for him.

Jack's face flushed with anger. "Why not?" She flicked her blonde hair off a shoulder.

"He is correct to not trust me. I would do the same," Teric tried to explain.

Ava shook her head at him, knowing Jack wouldn't find consolation in his words. She ushered Kanzo onto the bench next to Nerx and slid in beside him, making sure her thigh touched his. His body heat seeped through his armored pants, warming her, and sparking a flush of anticipation and arousal inside her.

"Now you're defending him?" Jack scowled at Teric.

Ava nodded. Yup, Teric's words weren't well-received. "Ulriq is protective of you, Jack. What's not to like?" She rested her hand on Kanzo's knee, squeezing it. When his breath hitched, she gifted him with an innocent smile.

"How would you feel if Kanzo listened in on your conversations?" Jack snapped.

"I have nothing to hide." Ava shrugged then jumped up to request hot chocolates from the rehydrator since it appeared as if Jack had no intention of appeasing Ulriq's curiosity. She also wanted Kanzo to try it. "Here we go, three hot chocolates with extra mini marshmallows." She slid the cups over to the men, flashing a happy smile to all. "Though I don't know where you'll put it. You would think burgers would fill you." She offered Aala a bowl of mini marshmallows in enough quantity for Teric to share before resuming her seat.

Nerx took the first sniff and sip. His expression was one of amazement. "Alodon. This is incredible." He gulped another mouthful, moaned then graced Ava with the biggest smile.

She blinked, finding herself stunned at his changed mood. Ulriq followed suit, took a sip, and within seconds was whispering something to Jack. Judging by her friend's flushed face, it was something sexual. Ava glanced at Kanzo. Only then did he take a sip before dipping to brush his mouth over hers, transferring the chocolate to her. She hummed before stealing another kiss.

"You taste better than this chocolate." Kanzo's unflinching gaze fluttered her heart-beat.

"You do know we have advanced hearing?" Nerx's comment drew her attention.

"And an excellent sense of smell." Jack gave Nerx a pointed look.

His nostrils flared, and he groaned. "Alodon's hell, females." He glowered at Ulriq. Not saying another word, he stormed over to the rehydrator, ordered another hot chocolate, and left the common.

"That was unkind, Jack," Teric said before releasing his laughter. It thundered as his shoulders shook. Ava smiled at Teric's amusement. He rumbled like a huge teddy bear.

"His holier-than-thou attitude gets annoying," Jack said with a dismissive flick of her hand. "Should I apologize, my Eth?"

Ulriq stared at her upturned face, his gaze caressing her features in adoration. "No," he said, his voice hoarse. "He is correct though. Your scent is evocative."

"You never complained before." Jack threw the accusation at Teric.

"You were not aroused, but now I do not scent you at all." Teric smiled. "I only scent my Dar Eth."

"Where is Vicky?" Jack glanced around the common, searching for their sister.

"She comms a human male...Antoine?"

"So, let me get this straight, excellent hearing and sense of smell?" Ava shoved a fry into her mouth before offering one to Kanzo. "And well-hung?" she teased, darting a glance at Jack, who blushed clear to her hairline. Ava giggled. "There's my innocent Jack."

"Are you speaking about my...?" Ulriq gaped in disbelief, the horror on his face called forth another chuckle from Ava. It felt good to laugh.

Jack patted Ulriq's hand before focusing on Ava. "I hope to limp tomorrow, are you planning on doing the same?"

When Ava's cheeks caught alight, Jack grinned. Tit for tat, and round one to Jack.

"Limp?" Kanzo asked Ava, lacing his fingers through hers and rested their clasped hands on his knee. "I know this word but not in this context."

"It means so much sex that I can't walk tomorrow."

Kanzo grumbled as his fingers twitched around her hand. Oh. Her heart lurched and heat pooled lower. She loved his reaction. Perhaps she'd scored on this round, after all.

Chapter Twenty-Four

The following morning, Ava went to the common in the hopes of finding Danic. She was in luck. She took full advantage of it, storming across to where Danic and Aaro sat, ignoring everyone else.

"I need your help, Danic." She slid onto the bench opposite him.

"Greetings, Ava," Danic said around a mouthful of meat.

"Okay, let's do pleasantries." She harumphed and flashed him a fake smile. "Hello, Danic, Aaro. How are you this morning? I need your help."

"I am not assisting until you answer a few questions."

She glared at Danic for this and darted her gaze around the room. What she had planned, Kanzo couldn't find out about, not yet. She indicated by hand gesture that she was waiting.

"How are you feeling?" Danic asked, for once his jovial expression absent.

"I'm well."

He raised an eyebrow in disbelief. "Still feeling guilty about Billy?"

"No." She graced him with a genuine smile. "I no longer have that crushing feeling." She pressed her palm to her sternum, indicating where that feeling had once resided. "Thank you for bringing Jack back to me, Danic. I think if she was…" Ava sucked in a breath before continuing past the lump in her throat. "I would've shattered."

"Kanzo would have caught you."

She nodded. Her Eth had been there for her every step of this adventure. "Yes, he would've."

At her words, Danic stood up. "So, what do you need?"

"Not here, the viewing deck." She glanced at Aaro. "You might as well come with us, Aaro. I might need you too." The silence stretched between them while she preceded them to the viewing deck. As soon as Aaro sat on the built-in bench, she faced them.

"Kanzo is stubborn. He is suffering from what we call blue balls." She waited for the O.D.I. to instruct them.

Aaro frowned. "It is worse than that, Ava. Self-gratification does not ease the pain. Only his Dar Eth can bring him relief."

"It's as I thought. I have to get him off?" She gritted her teeth, ignoring her burning cheeks at the strangest conversation instigated by her.

Both men sighed as they waited for their O.D.I. to explain.

"You need to do more than get him off." Danic grinned.

"Okay, then you have to sneak me into his barracks, slip me in and out of his quarters too."

"What are you planning to do?" Danic jerked back. "You do know that females are not allowed in the barracks?"

"Which is why I need your help." She rolled her eyes at him. "I need to consummate our marriage. To save Kanzo like he saved me." She gave a determined nod. They blinked at her as if her words confused them. Or perhaps her motivation did? "I mean to have his dick in me." She spelled out for them, ignoring the heat that warmed her neck.

"Alodon's balls, Ava." Aaro's pinched his brow.

Danic laughed and leaned against the bulkhead. "Once you give yourself to him, he will become addicted to you and only you."

Her mouth dropped open at his warning. "Addicted? In what way?"

"To your scent, your touch, your voice. That is the true power of the Ethera. Were you an Etterian female, the addiction would be mutual," he said.

"But because I'm human, you don't know whether I'll become addicted to him?" They nodded. "Jack does act addicted..." Ava remembered Vicky mentioning her attempts to get Jack to remove Ulriq's tunic.

"It is why Kanzo is waiting. The Ethera will demand he claim you more than once over many days."

Aaro made no sense. She frowned. "Why over many days?" *Like a honeymoon of sorts?*

"Because a female can only accommodate a male once a day," Danic said as if she was the idiot.

"If that female is not human." Ava folded her arms across her chest. "Our males are like your females, whereas our females are like your males." She gave them a pointed look.

Excitement lightened Aaro's indigo eyes. "And you find fulfillment every time?"

She froze. What was she thinking? Yes, she wasn't a virgin anymore but that didn't mean she could entice a man, even if Kanzo would be half-asleep. "Do you think I can seduce him?" she whispered.

"Maker." Aaro threw up his arms in frustration. "One moment you're demanding, then you're crude, and now you're timid? Etterian males lack the necessary knowledge to handle such a variety of emotions. And if what you say is true...about your females' fulfillments..." He growled.

"Ava..." Danic glared Aaro into silence. "Kanzo trembles at your touch."

He does. She grinned. "As do I when he touches me."

"We will ensure you have access and privacy en route." Danic pushed off the bulkhead. "You handle the easy part."

"Easy? How do you sneak up on an Etterian, Danic?" She rested her hands on her hips.

"Carefully," he said as he sauntered off the deck.

She snorted then glanced at Aaro, waiting for him to advise her.

"He should be asleep. So, if he moves, freeze, stop breathing. You will be fortunate if he does not scent you first."

"Shit," she said. "Am I insane to attempt this, Aaro?"

He stared at her for a moment, his gaze traveling over her features. "Your efforts are appreciated, Ava." He strode off, abandoning her to her wayward thoughts.

"Cryptic bastards," she muttered.

Chapter Twenty-Five

Etterian Battleship, Kushin
Speeding toward Earth
Ava and Vicky's Quarters

Ulriq drew in a deep breath as he paused outside the girls' shared quarters. Everything he needed was in place. This was the final hurdle. As much as he adored Jack, he found other human females unpredictable. With a grimace, he requested entry and waited.

"Ulriq? Where's Jack?" Vicky asked in alarm as she opened the door.

He stepped into their quarters, forcing her to shift aside to avoid him. Once the door closed behind him, he lowered his shoulders, hoping to not intimidate these females.

"She sleeps," he said. "Jack is well, but I must speak to her girls."

"About?" Ava assumed a comfy.

Ulriq studied her for a moment, her dark skin, her bold expression from those exquisite green eyes. Yes, he could see why the Yithians had thought her a half-breed Etterian. "I wish to give Jack this wedding day she desires."

They gasped, their faces morphing from shock to excited delight. Such an emotive species. It was why the Ethera's choice of females pleased Xeus.

"You do? Oh, this is wonderful. And is this a surprise?" Ava flashed Vicky a grin.

"Yes."

"You'll sweep Jack off her feet." Vicky's voice rose with anticipation.

"Sweep off her feet?" Ulriq scowled. What a strange custom. "I saw no mention of a broom in the annals." He raised his wrist to message Prex. Perhaps he'd missed something during the research.

"It's not literal, Ulriq," Ava said. "You're sweeping her into your arms and off her feet to carry into a forever-in-love future."

"I understand." He didn't, but he wasn't prepared to waste more time with them than he needed to.

"What did you have in mind, Ulriq?" Vicky bounced on her heels with ill-contained excitement.

"I have asked for her hand in marriage from Fred and Mich as per the wedding guidelines Pilot Ksal secured for me." The girls released blissful sighs. Ulriq ignored them, not understanding their reaction to his words. "It is the white garment that poses a problem. I assume it is something she needs to approve of?"

"The wedding dress?" Ava squeaked to which Ulriq nodded.

"I suppose if we all tried on dresses…," Vicky said.

Ava tapped her chin. "We can ask Fred to say he wanted to walk us down the aisle, and now that we're leaving Earth, he'll never get the chance."

"That could work. Dresses cost a fortune, though," Vicky said.

"Cost is of no importance," Ulriq said, and it wasn't, not for his Jack. Whatever she needed, it was his duty, his honor to provide it.

"You cannot be that wealthy," Ava said.

Ulriq brushed aside Ava's disbelief. "We have personal tokens. Regardless of this, what Etterians need, Etteria provides."

"Wedding dresses for all of us, it is." Ava danced in her comfy, her eagerness reaching him.

"But where to hold it? Cromdon Park seems the best location. I'll propose we picnic there with baskets from Antoine." Vicky laughed. "I'm brilliant if I don't say so myself."

"Picnic?" Ulriq scowled. His O.D.I. hurried to inform him, but the images made no sense. "No, not food." He wouldn't tolerate a further delay. He needed Jack to acknowledge she was his beyond the physical relationship they shared. She wasn't Etterian nor was she familiar with the lore surrounding the Ethera. In her mind, she wasn't Ulriq's, not in any official capacity. "Jack is mine, but I must wait?"

"Okay, so a rush wedding." Ava chuckled. "Got it. We'll *pretend* there's a picnic. You can take her home straight after the vows."

"I am grateful. This is a better solution." Ulriq forced a smile.

"Will you wear a tux?" Ava's gaze traveled the length of him in a calculating manner. He didn't like the perusal. It made him...uncomfortable.

"I need to wear something now?" Alodon's balls. What next? How much more did he need to do to see this wedding done?

"Yes, as a bridegroom. It's traditional to wear a tuxedo." Vicky clasped her hands in her lap. "And with a matching cumber band, perhaps the bowtie, as well."

"That's too much for Ulriq to have to remember. Just ask for a tux, and it'll be enough." Ava nudged Taylor on the shoulder.

"Then I shall wear it. Anything for Jack." He raised his wrist and opened a new message for Prex, but Ava grabbed his arm to type on his holographic buttons. He didn't like her scent, not that it was offensive. It just wasn't Jack's.

She stepped back, and Vicky hurried to stand beside her. Both females sighed at him, again. Their eyes seemed manic, despite their bright smiles.

"And a preacher to marry you?" Vicky asked.

"Fred indicated that he will assume responsibility for this," Ulriq said. "Is there anything else I might have missed?"

They shook their heads, and their manic expressions sparked to life. Had Ulriq been on a battlefield against such an opponent, he might have cut them down without hesitation. Something was disquieting about their joyful eyes.

Beating a hasty retreat, he left them whispering to each other, their excitement still palpable. Having their support was imperative. He typed on his O.D.I. and strode to the viewing deck. When he walked in, it was to find Kanzo and Teric awaiting him as per his missive. He detailed his plan, explaining the human females' need for such a day and all it entailed.

"Truly?" Kanzo frowned. He shared a need to please his Dar Eth. Ulriq nodded, satisfied to see the male accepting his gift, at last.

"My Victoria has not mentioned this to me." Teric scowled.

"Regardless, I wish to provide such a day for my Dar Eth. This will necessitate your participation, as well."

"As you require, Ulriq," Kanzo said.

"You are to wear a tux. Please request that your Dar Eths assist you in this. Michel will be my guide. I will communicate further details via your O.D.I." Ulriq had a slight bounce in his step when he left the viewing deck. Yes, joy did warm his chest, for he'd accomplished the final hurdle to *sweeping* Jack off her feet. Now, he need only wait the two days until they reached Earth.

Chapter Twenty-Six

Etterian Battleship, Kushin
Speeding toward Earth
Her quarters.

AVA WAITED OUTSIDE HER door at 0600 when Kanzo strode toward her. He took the time to admire her in her running garments, wishing he could do more than look. She scented sweet as if she'd cleansed with her hair gathered on top of her head in a long tail. He wanted to twist it in his fist and tug her head back to ravage her mouth. Drawing in a deep breath, he folded his arms across his chest to hide his trembling hands.

"Good morning," she said with a bright smile, her eyes alight with excitement and nervousness.

"Good morning, *thamani*," he said. "I have found a suitable running area. Come with me." He strode down the passage, listening for her small footsteps.

When she followed, he smiled, pleased that she trusted him. Fifteen minutes later, he paused in front of a sealed door. He scanned his O.D.I. over the sigil. This was the correct door. It opened with lighting illuminating the inside as he'd requested. "This is a service passage. It follows the outer walls of the battleship. We do not waste resources to power the lighting when not in use. Would this be suitable?"

She peered through the door, looking both ways before blessing him with a pleased smile. "Yes, it's wonderful, Kanzo."

He stepped in behind her and closed the air-door, sealing it. The quiet was oppressive, but he didn't care, not with her there. She hung a towel over an exposed metal pipe. Then she did leg stretches, explaining to him why each warm-up was necessary. She demonstrated her excellent fitness level, her flexibility. He tried not to stare as her leg muscles rippled beneath her leggings, but he couldn't help himself.

She broke into a run, letting him trail her as and when he was ready and at his own pace. He wished he could take the time to savor her consideration. It gave him hope. He wanted…no, needed to kiss her, needed to hold her. Fighting off the Ethera was becoming harder with each passing day. He couldn't ignore it, no matter how hard he tried.

He ran, his gaze focused on Ava in front of him. His feet thumped on the grated flooring, echoing off the narrow passage. He straggled on purpose. To watch her run was a pleasure, with her backside swaying encased in those skin-tight leggings, with her hair swinging from side-to-side, her bare waist revealing all that skin, tempting him to touch. He imagined tasting her, or perhaps untying her hair, to see it spread across his chest, his stomach, and lower. Grabbing hold of his thinning control, he focused on the task. He kept pace, realizing how wonderful the footwear was since he was certain his boots would have hurt him by now. The garments she ordered for him were comfortable and unrestrictive.

By the third cycle around the battleship, his legs were on fire. They'd run for at least an hour. Sweat sheened his body, and he was breathless. Not that he would stop. He was starting to understand her joy, the freedom, the time alone with his thoughts. Running required a different set of muscles than greatsword wielding and general Gika hunting. By the time she stopped, her skin glistened with perspiration, and her scent was musky. He suspected it was how she'd scent after a night of fulfillment.

She gasped for air as she did other exercises. He groaned but mimicked her movements, assuming these new exercises were as important. He was content to watch her stretch, to admire how she twisted her body into suggestive positions.

"Now for breakfast." She bounced as if energy still coursed through her.

Nodding, he opened the air-door and gestured to her to step through.

"And water." He sealed the door behind them and deactivated the lighting. Pleased with himself for having survived that, to have shared in this experience with her, he led the way to her quarters.

"How was it?" Vicky asked from a comfy as soon as they entered.

"Kanzo did very well," Ava said.

Warmth swelled within his chest, joyful that she thought so. Despite the need to hold her, he watched as she jogged to the rehydrator to order two bottles of water. She tossed him one.

"Wow." Vicky grinned. "Well done, Kanzo." She jumped up, placed her cup in the waste disposal, and headed for the door. "See you later. Off to have breakfast with Teric and Aala."

"My legs are burning, but I enjoyed it," he said to Ava as he dropped into a comfy to finish his water.

"They're burning?" Her brow furrowed.

She tapped something into the replicator and approached him carrying a bottle with a light golden substance inside.

"Roll up your shorts," she said.

He did so, curious as to her intentions. She stared at his exposed thighs. Her breath hitched then her heart altered its rhythm. He glanced at his thighs and wondered why the sight of them affected her.

"Shift forward on the comfy for me," she said, her voice rough, and he did so. She poured oil on her hands and rubbed his calf and thigh muscles.

He stiffened, surprised at her touch, at the strength in her fingers. But within minutes he was moaning. His muscles no longer stung as he melted into the comfy. She focused on his other leg. Her tongue pressed to her top lip in concentration. He tried to think other thoughts, certain that an arousal in these thin garments would be as if he stood before her naked.

She stopped torturing him with her touch and gathered the bottle to place on the table before disappearing into the cleansing room to wash the oil from her hands.

"Thank you," he said when she entered the room.

"Breakfast?"

Nodding, he accepted the towel she tossed at him. He wiped the oil from his legs while she brought their food over. "What is this?"

Ava dropped into a comfy beside him, balancing two plates. She offered one to him.

"Bacon, egg, and cheese toasted sandwich." She took a huge bite of her own.

He bit into his, moaning at the rich salty flavor, and hastily devoured the tiny triangle.

"What are your plans for today?" she asked between mouthfuls.

"I have no plans."

"Want to watch a movie with me?" She paused mid-bite.

"An entertainment vid?" He would watch the passing stars with her as long she was near.

"Yes, if you have a few hours to spare."

He blinked. Was she asking him to spend the day with her? Alodon's balls. This pleased him.

"I have time," he said, almost overwhelmed by the bright smile she blessed him with. "Thank you for sharing your running with me."

"I won't say my pleasure. Tomorrow morning you might be a little stiff," she said. "If you are, come to me and I'll rub it better." Her eyes went wide, and her cheeks trembled.

He stilled. "What is the matter, my Ava?"

"I just remembered you might feel worse two days from now." She jumped up to dispose of her plate, reaching over to take his plate too.

He let her but rose to follow her, frowning at her. "Ava?"

Her shoulders slumped then she faced him. "My words have a different meaning. It was unintentional, Kanzo, I swear."

He replayed her words. Rub something stiff? A chuckle rumbled from his chest and up his throat. "You offered to rub my malehood, and only if it is stiff?"

Her embarrassment traveled down her lovely neck. She glanced at the floor as if doing so hid her face from him. He caught her hand and used it to bring her into his arms. Lifting her chin with his finger, he forced her to meet his gaze.

"*Thamani*, I did not hear your words as you imagined. I heard only your concern." He dipped to hold his mouth against hers, but because he couldn't restrain himself, he claimed her mouth. His tongue delved in and tasted her, the salty rich flavor of bacon and cheese still on her lips. He moaned and drank from her as if he were a dying male. Maker, he needed her.

He grasped her backside, filling his palms with her softness. Crushing her body against his, he kept her pinned to him. Their garments were too thin for his control to handle. Her softness and pebbled nipples brushed his chest as if they were naked. The sweet musky scent of her deepened, and he growled, needing more.

Trailing his hands up her back, over her bare midriff, he gripped the fabric of her tight tunic. With a tug, the fabric surrendered to his forceful and determined fingers. He could now peel the tunic forward, bearing her breasts to his hungry gaze. She moaned into his mouth but didn't stop him. Instead, she lowered her arms to allow the ruined garment to fall to the floor. As soon as it slipped past her fingertips, she grabbed his muscled upper arms and pressed her body against his.

Abandoning reason, he lifted her to slide her backside onto the replicator. He stepped between her parted knees and captured her nipple into his mouth, sucking it hard. A hoarse sound tore from her, rising from the back of her throat as she arched in response to the heat and force of his mouth, thrusting her breast into his face. He rumbled his approval before looping an arm around her bare back.

The taste of her nipple across his tongue, the scent of her arousal in his nostrils, the feel of her soft skin under his fingers; he couldn't last any longer, and didn't want to. He needed her, needed her touch, needed to bury himself inside her. He released her nipple with a deep groan then crushed her to him as he fought for control, his breathing shallow, his body shuddering.

"Just two more days," he said.

"Kanzo?" Her voice rasped across his senses.

He groaned again, and his arms spasmed around her. She rubbed his shoulders as if to offer him comfort. Her touch excited him, but that she thought to soothe him was what he appreciated.

"Why can't we ask Nerx for another Officer's quarters?" she asked.

He groaned and leaned back to smile at her. At the sight of her beautiful unbound breasts, he shut his eyes and crushed her to him again. Maker.

"Wait." She pushed against his chest. He stepped back. She jumped off the replicator to order a new shirt. "Okay, I'm decent."

He opened his eyes to find she'd pulled on a loose tunic for which he was grateful.

"We should have asked earlier. It is pointless now."

Sighing, she picked up her ruined top. She placed it in the waste disposal before facing him.

"May we watch a vid another day?" he asked.

The breath-taking smile she bestowed upon him dispelled his anxiety.

"Go do what you need to do, my Eth."

He squeezed her hand, pressed a kiss to her forehead, and darted out of her room. A few sparring rounds in the common might restore his control. He messaged Danic on his O.D.I.

Chapter Twenty-Seven

Etterian Battleship, Kushin
Speeding toward Earth
Kanzo's Quarters

Ava's fingers trembled where she gripped Kanzo's door frame. She drew in a deep breath, cast a glance down the abandoned passage of the barracks, and slipped into Kanzo's quarters, more nervous than she'd been in her life. Undressing, she lowered her clothes to the floor. Etterians didn't allow females in the barracks, and she didn't want to know who'd given her security access. Pilot Ksal or Data Officer Prex? She gritted her teeth, not wanting to think about all the males who knew she was here to offer her body to Kanzo, to seduce her husband. She winced.

When Kanzo had darted away from her this morning, she'd messaged Danic that this would happen tonight. And here she stood. She didn't know how she was going to make it to Kanzo's bed without him hearing her. There was no escaping this, now that she'd involved the entire battleship. Oh, how cunning her mind was. She sighed and squared her shoulders. After the incident this morning, she couldn't sit by and allow him to remain in pain when it wasn't necessary.

She raised her foot and placed it with care, then the other, creeping toward his bed in the corner. As she approached, he moved, stirring the blanket. She froze, not certain what she would do if he woke up. Panic gripped her with her heart leaping into her throat. She held her breath and waited. But instead of sitting up and demanding an explanation, he shoved out a bare leg. She gaped, and drooled, staring at the muscled length of his leg. Making love to her husband wouldn't be a hardship. She smiled at the rush of heat to the juncture of her thighs. When he didn't move again, she released her breath on a slow exhale and inched forward until she reached his bed.

At his bare chest, the indents of his abs, his narrow waist, the way his mouth parted, she shivered. Her heartbeat pounded in her ears, and she was more nervous now that she faced the reality of her plan. She stood before him naked and was about to climb onto his bed. She cursed herself. What kind of desperate woman was she? An aroused one. She huffed, then clapped a hand over her mouth.

Clenching her fists, she lowered herself to lie alongside him, placing her head on the pillow next to his. Gathering her courage, she rubbed her mouth across his. A hint of his breath made hers catch. He mumbled in his sleep. She stroked his face and pressed her mouth to his. He groaned and snaked his arm around her, pulling her closer to him.

"Ava." He moaned into her mouth, though his eyes remained shut.

"Kanzo," she said.

This time his eyes fluttered open. "Am I dreaming?" he asked in a rough yet sensual voice as his hand traveled from her hip and up her back, his touch almost reverent.

"Kiss me, Kanzo." She held her mouth to his again but licked his bottom lip.

He grumbled and crushed her to his length, trapping the blanket between them. His mouth slashed over hers, his tongue swooping in, to taste her, to learn every inch of her. She moaned at the velvet feel of him. His touch burned a path to her bare ass to grasp a cheek, sending shards of need through her.

He groaned but jerked back. "Ava, what are you doing here?" He blinked at her, then his gaze dipped, his eyes widening. He feathered kisses along her jaw to her throat to her collarbone.

"I can leave," she said, breathless under his intense onslaught.

"Never." He rolled onto his back and pulled her on top of him. "You are never leaving me now that I have you in my arms." He gripped her ass, trapping her against him.

Heat pooled between her thighs, and she arched her back, crying out at the need burning through her. He pulled her up, using his hands on her ass as leverage. Her breasts thrust into his face, and with a blissful sigh from him, he nipped a taut nipple. A groan vibrated up his throat and into her nipple sucked deep into his mouth.

"Vow to me, Ava," he said as he brushed kisses to the other nipple. He swirled his tongue around it, refusing to suck it until she promised.

"Kanzo, please." She wasn't afraid to plead for what she wanted, and she needed his mouth on her.

"Vow it, Ava."

She whimpered as he clenched and unclenched her ass, making her hips swirl in reaction. "I promise," she said. "I promise, Kanzo."

He sucked her nipple so deep into his mouth that shards of heat shot straight from there to her core. She thrashed, loving the feel of his hot mouth on her, his touch intimate. Her fingers fluttered over his face, down to his shoulders where she scraped her fingernails before leaning back with a knee on either side of his hips. The hard length of him rubbed her through the blanket. She took a moment to rotate her hips, gyrating her sex across his dick.

He hissed. Her heart fluttered at his reaction, sparking a blissful wave of joy.

"Ava." He touched her at the apex of her thighs while shoving the blankets down.

She gasped at his seeking fingers, but still managed to lift her hips, giving him enough space to push the blankets aside. His arousal sprung free, large and hungry. She lowered her hips to rub her sex along the granite length of him as his fingers teased her to higher peaks of need. Her purr was breathless, mindless, as sensations battered her body. He licked and nipped her nipples, the sharp tugs making her cry out as his deft fingers drove her wild. He halted, withdrawing his fingers, and she whimpered her disappointment. Only to watch him suck on a finger, to taste her.

It was the sexiest thing she'd ever seen. The way his eyes closed, his lips wrapping around his finger. A growl followed a pleased expression before he opened his ice-blue eyes to meet her gaze. He lifted her hips high enough for the head of his arousal to brush at her entrance. Her mouth parted in delight, and she lowered herself onto him, needing that contact, his length inside her. Her mewls of pleasure mingled with his. His fingers gripped her hips, eager to rush her, eager to slow her. The girth of him stretching her parted her mouth in awe.

"Maker," he rasped. When he'd buried himself to the hilt, he paused, his hands cupping her face as he dusted reverent kisses across her skin. "*Thamani*, I have you, and you're mine." He sipped from her lips, and despite the ache in her core, his expression thumped her heart into a new rhythm. There was something intense in his gaze, as if she was his moon and stars. It was a heady feeling, one that swelled her chest with breathtaking warmth.

His body shuddered, drawing her to the moment. She slid her channel along the length of him before impaling herself on him again. His breath caught with every impalement, his reactions unguarded and filled with joy. Sensations skittered from her breasts to her throbbing core.

"Kanzo." She scraped her nails over his nipples, then she arched to capture a kiss.

He circled his arms around her waist and flipped her onto her back, burying himself a little deeper. Gasping, she raised her legs, digging her heels into his backside, encouraging him. He withdrew and thrust into her, chanting her name between breaths.

"Harder, faster, please, Kanzo." She thrashed from side-to-side, and when he complied, she arched right off the bed to scream his name. His length filled her to the maximum, a completion settling on her as the tingling intensified to an unbearable level. The wave crested, and she cried out, whispering his name, begging him not to stop.

She exploded, splintering into shards so small she couldn't piece herself back together, not without his help. Not that she cared at that moment. He pounded into her, the constant friction spurred another climb, too unexpected she forgot to breathe. Shivers rolled over her, making her scream his name, her nipples tingled and hardened to stone, her womb clenched, and her hips rose, demanding he take her, own her. A flush covered her body as she floated down to the bed from her trip to the stars.

He buried his face in his pillow and roared his orgasm. The most incredible sensation flowed through her as if her body was liquid fire. He collapsed on top of her, though carrying the brunt of his weight on his elbows. He didn't withdraw from her. She was glad of it, not wanting him to move, and was content to die like that.

He stared at her, once again cupping her face to press kisses to her temple, along the bridge of her nose before capturing her mouth for a soul-wrenching kiss. He buried his fingers in her hair and sighed.

"I do not want to leave you." He graced her with a sweet smile, revealing his dimples.

"Then don't." She twitched her hips, surprised to find him still hard. Her eyelids fluttered at the sensations her small movements made. She did it again and moaned, arched her back on a purr and brushed her nipples against his chest in the process. Her core spasmed, and her eyes opened to meet his. "You are still hard, Kanzo."

"I am always aroused around you, Ava." His breath warmed her earlobe just as he swirled his tongue along it before nipping it.

She gasped. "You can go again?" Damn, she hoped so, because, after one session, she was addicted.

"I am an Etterian male," he said as if that explained it. It didn't.

"I'm a human woman. I can go many times." She swirled her hips, teasing at the length of him.

"Truth?" His eyes widened, so beautiful a pale blue against the bronze of his skin. He grinned, withdrawing his entire length before thrusting into her. She cried out her pleasure, burying her fingernails into his back.

"So good," she rasped, a new swell of sensations laying claim to her.

The man was well hung so the adage was true. But instead of pounding into her, the way she needed, he moved slow and deliberately, withdrawing then sliding in. He kissed her, conquering her mouth with his hips thrusting and one hand toying with her nipple.

"Kanzo?" she whined.

"I know you need me to claim you, *thamani*. But I cannot bring myself to do so. I have found my fulfillment, now I wish to take my pleasure." He feathered kisses along her jaw to her ear then down to press an open-mouthed kiss to her neck. "For so long, I have dreamed of adoring you." He feathered kisses along her collarbone before cherishing a breast and its taut nipple.

She thrashed in reaction to his tender ministrations, the heat of his mouth on her skin, the feel of him still buried deep within her. And when he moved his fingers to brush across her curls to tease her, her hips lifted off the bed, threatening to throw him off. She wasn't strong enough to do so, but his laughter was husky as he tormented her. A burning sensation began where his fingers touched. Then he latched onto her nipple, and with his fingers teasing her, the triple onslaught had her arching her back, a deep purr at the back of her throat. Just before he gave the final flick of his fingers, he withdrew his arousal and slammed into her, driving her into the abyss of sensation and pleasure.

She screamed, and to her delight, he roared as he too orgasmed. His torso merged with hers, his weight unbearable yet relished. She knew not where he began, and she ended. He flipped her leg over so that he could remain buried within her, then collapsed onto the bed. He pulled her into the curve of his body, holding her against his chest.

"Do you want to go again?" she asked a few minutes later as she snuggled into his embrace.

"I want to hold you, *thamani*." He nuzzled her hair with his chin to expose the nape of her neck, placing a kiss there. He drew in a deep breath as if he sniffed her. Her fingertips traced unknown patterns over his forearm trapping her, just below her breasts. He toyed with her unbound hair, stroking and curling strands around his fingers. She sighed, content to let sleep lull her.

Kanzo's Quarters

The following morning.

Kanzo sensed Ava drift off to sleep and smiled, realizing the warmth in his chest was...happiness. His arm buzzed, and he scowled at the intrusion, but he activated the message, nevertheless. Laughter rumbled from his belly which he managed to keep low enough so as not to disturb her.

Nerx had to evacuate the barracks because Kanzo found his fulfillment like a rutting kreso. Kanzo chuckled at the image of the overly hairy, odorous wild animal rutting. And happily so, he responded to Nerx. Still grinning to himself, he wrapped his body around hers and allowed sleep to claim him.

The buzzing up his arm woke him, and he grumbled his displeasure. As he climbed out of the depths of sleep, having had the most incredible dreams, he focused on his surroundings. Softness filled his arms. A tight wet heat wrapped around his arousal, and it pulsed, making him throb with need. A sweet musky scent teased his nose, and he inhaled to appease the tickle. He knew that scent.

Said softness shifted and rubbed along the length of him. His eyelids flew open to meet the sleepy green gaze of his Dar Eth.

"Morning," she said before twisting to kiss him.

"I did not dream this?" He gaped then cringed, feeling like a fool.

"It was better than a dream." She smiled then moved as if to un-impale herself.

Growling, he pulled out before flipping her onto her back. He rose onto his knees to settle between her thighs.

"Remind me," he said, his voice guttural, then he claimed her mouth with a kiss.

Chapter Twenty-Eight

Earth

Just Outside Town

Mrs. Hastings Home for Happy Children

AVA RUSHED INTO THE large house, eager to see everyone, to see Olivia who'd taken over when Mrs. Hastings had died in her sleep. Ava peeked at Kanzo. He smiled, jogged up to her, and wrapped an arm around her. Leaning down, he kissed her then faced the house.

"We are not alone," he chuckled.

She shushed him with a finger to his lips. "I tell you, Kanzo, if it wasn't for you, I'd kiss each boy in the house. Thank you for saving them," she said louder than usual, winking at Kanzo, hoping he'd play along.

"I am pleased to hear this, Ava, for I would have to challenge the male who dares to steal my female's kisses from me," he said with a pretend chest thump.

For someone who'd never been around children, his response was perfect. She flashed him a lustful look, promising him something special later. His smile curled into a full grin, revealing two dimples. "Keep smiling at me like that, *thamani*, and we may not make it inside," he said, his voice taking on a husky note.

"Ava?" Olivia opened the door, revealing a few children in the foyer listening in. "Where've you been? What happened?"

"Olivia, come meet my husband." Ava bounced forward to grab Olivia's hand, pulling her toward Kanzo. Yes, *her* husband. A thrill shot through her, and she gave him a delighted smile. They spent too much time in his quarters, but she didn't mind. The male without the Ethera pressing on him was sweet and considerate.

"Husband?" Olivia gaped at Kanzo.

Ava watched his reaction. Though the Ethera was definitive, the sight of Olivia's lilac eyes would make any male swoon. He stared into her eyes for a moment longer than needed, but when he looked at Ava, his expression softened. Butterflies exploded in her chest, sparking a wave of hope that he might love her.

"Kanzo, this is Olivia. She runs the orphanage." Ava raced toward the children, needing to escape the strong emotions fighting for supremacy in her heart. "The first person I see gets a kiss."

Grabbing Mikey, she planted a wet one on his cheek, loving the gagging noises he faked. Gathering up the twins, she gave them each a kiss. Tommy dodged her fingers, hiding behind little Maddie, whom Ava scooped into her arms to kiss and tickle. Even grumpy Neve didn't escape her hugs and kisses. With a sigh, she hugged Saira, holding her arms out to look at her, before hugging her again. She hugged Ruby before turning her to meet Kanzo. A pat on her leg had her smiling at Lily.

"And me?"

"I didn't forget you, Lily. I always save you for last and for the longest of kisses." And she scooped her up, giving her a big squeeze and a long, exaggerated kiss with fake noises.

"I missed you, Ava. I thought you left me," the little girl said as she raised her tiny face to Ava's.

"Never, sweetheart." Ava kissed her temple before turning to her audience. "Boy, do I have a story to tell you."

"Storytime?" Tommy risked coming closer now that Ava had her arms full.

At her nod, they scurried to the lounge, finding their usual spots, while she sat in the large wilted armchair with Lily still in her lap. Ava told them in embellished detail how nasty sharks stole her and how she met the shark king, and the yellow squid bought her from the king. She spun it that Kanzo charged in, weapon in hand to rescue her. She told them, that when her knees weakened, she knew he was the male for her. Then she married him on the spot. They gaped at him. He shifted on his feet as if their worship made him uncomfortable. Although, the smile he bestowed on Ava took her breath away.

"Did the yellow squid buy you 'cos you're too beautiful?" Lily asked and snuck a glance at Kanzo.

Ava held her breath.

"Yes, he did, *minus susa*," Kanzo said. "He wanted to keep Ava and not let me have her."

"Did you cut off his tentacles with your sword?" Mikey jumped up to swish his imaginary sword from side-to-side, with sounds included. Kanzo threw back his head and laughed a great and booming sound, surprising Lily, who cowered against Ava.

"I wish I could have, but I could not have my female see that," Kanzo said, still smiling before he kneeled before Ava. He held out his long-fingered hand to Lily as one would to a stray dog. Ava didn't have the heart to tell him that the sight of his large hand wouldn't calm a frightened child. "I did not mean to scare you, *minus susa*. I am big, therefore, my laugh is big. But I can also be gentle."

He stroked a finger along Ava's arm, showing Lily that he wouldn't harm her. Ava gasped, surprised at how gentle his large hand could be. Lily held out her scarred arm for Kanzo to stroke. He did so, before tapping her nose, bringing forth a bright smile from her.

"You have long hair like a girl," Tommy said.

"Not for a warrior. The longer our hair, the more honor we have," Kanzo said.

"A girl does not have all those muscles, silly," twelve-year-old Neve said.

"I'm not silly," Tommy grumbled.

"Juice time," Olivia called and ushered the children into the kitchen. Even Lily scampered off Ava's lap, leaving Ava alone with Kanzo, Saira, and Ruby.

"Did that happen, Angel?" Saira asked, her gray eyes large in her face. She peeked at Kanzo.

"Everything except the sword fighting." Ava grinned. "Kanzo's prince bought me from the Maloidian Ambassador."

"And you're smiling?" Ruby asked aghast then huffed a deep red curl out of her startling dark blue eyes. "I would've been terrified."

"I was when it happened. Then I was rescued with an awesome story to tell, and I have Kanzo now. He keeps me safe."

The two girls studied Kanzo.

He grinned and tugged Ava out of the chair, just to wrap his arms around her. She sighed, needing his touch, as well. That it showed how much he adored her was also good. Olivia walked in and smiled at them before she collapsed into an armchair, exhaustion circling her eyes.

"How are things? Need anything?" Ava asked from within his arms. When she tapped him, he released her, and she dropped to the floor at Olivia's feet.

"You are married now, Angel. It's time to worry about your own home."

"Out with it," Ava said, her tone brooking no argument.

"They are repossessing the house on Monday," Olivia said.

"Those bastards." Ava clenched her jaw, trying to keep from venting her anger. "You can have my house. It's not as big as this one, but it's fully paid off."

"Where would you stay?" Saira squeaked.

"With Kanzo on his battleship."

"In space?" Ruby gasped. She studied Kanzo before nodding.

"You're leaving us?" Saira asked, tears forming and falling. A wail had her rushing out of the room, returning a minute later with baby Jessie in her arms. Kanzo blinked at the baby then at Saira. He grunted then crossed to Ava, pressed a kiss on her temple, and left through the front door.

"He's huge, Ava. Are you sure about this?" Ruby asked.

"Yes, so sure that I married him."

"Good. I like him so far. Billy wasn't the best choice for you," Ruby said.

Ava jerked back as if slapped. That Ruby would make such an observation startled her. Billy hadn't been the best choice, but she'd needed to feel loved, cherished, and in a way, he had made her feel all those things. That she'd also felt betrayal, sorrow, despair, those were emotions she hadn't asked for and no one deserved.

"Just don't put Kanzo on a pedestal. He's a man and fallible," Ruby said.

Ava hugged her, blinking back tears. "When did you become so wise, Ruby?"

"Where did he go?" Saira asked, cooing to baby Jessie.

Ava shrugged. "I don't know, but he'll tell me if it's important."

"He's talking to his arm." Olivia peered through the bay windows at Kanzo who stood outside on the mottled grass. "He's coming back." Color stained her cheeks as she faced forward.

Ava chuckled at Olivia's guilty expression and girlish behavior.

Kanzo strode into the house as if he owned it. He gestured to Ava and Olivia, indicating he needed a moment alone with them. Ava stepped away from Ruby and smiled at Olivia, shrugging as she followed Kanzo. The moment she joined him outside, he drew her into his arms. She was content to let him hold her, always.

"I have spoken to my king. He has offered you and your *damu* sanctuary on Etteria."

Olivia gasped, her mouth gaped, and her eyes widened.

Ava squealed, happiness cascading through her. Now she need not say goodbye. They could all come with her. She threw her arms around Kanzo, crushing him to her while she jumped up and down.

"You need never be concerned regarding sustenance, garments, safety, or their education," Kanzo said, but he spoke to Ava, his gaze resting on her face. He dipped his head to kiss her, calming her as nothing else could have.

"Are you serious?" Olivia sniffed, and a tear slipped out unhindered.

"It would mean relocating all of you." Ava shifted within his arms to face Olivia before she pressed a kiss to his bare shoulder.

"Which would've happened on Monday anyway. Now the kids can see it as an adventure." Olivia dabbed her eyes. "Thank you, Kanzo. To not worry, to have every need taken care of?" She paused to chew on her lip, darting a nervous glance at him. Ava knew that look. "Would I still have a say in their wellbeing?"

"Yes, though we would prefer to train them as we do our own *damu*, females included."

"I don't have much of a choice, not with Monday looming. I suppose changes to their education would be acceptable, after all, they may need to know certain skills to survive up there." Olivia nodded. "How much time do we have before we leave?"

"We have a picnic this afternoon, how about first thing tomorrow morning?" Ava glanced at Kanzo to see if that was all right.

"That is suitable." He tightened his arms. With Billy, she hadn't been demonstrative, but with Kanzo, she found it a natural reaction in his presence.

"Nine?" Olivia moaned. "I'm not sure we'll have everything packed."

Ava squeezed her hand. "Everything is taken care of: blankets, beds, clothes. The only thing you need to bring are keepsakes, and you don't have many of those."

Olivia paled then flushed. "You weren't kidding when you said everything." She smiled. "Very well, nine it is."

"You're not leaving?" Lily asked from the door.

Ava twisted to look at her and shook her head. "Not yet, sweetheart. Come, Lily."

Lily darted her large blue gaze at Kanzo, still startled at the size of him. Ava kneeled to throw her arms out wide. The little girl scurried into her embrace. She rose with her Lily-bundle squirming against her.

"I think someone is getting bigger...and heavier. Is Olivia feeding you rocks?" she teased to which Lily giggled.

"She calls them muffins." At Lily's words, Olivia blushed. Her baking tended to lean toward burnt but she persevered.

"That is my female you are hugging." Kanzo scooped Ava into his arms, carrying them both. It felt strange to be airborne, and that he handled their combined weight with such ease called forth a deeper appreciation of his strength, his body. Lily squealed in fright and grabbed onto Ava who'd thrown back her head and laughed as the world spun around her. She felt carefree and...cherished.

Seeing she was in no danger of falling, Lily giggled too. Then when Kanzo spun them around again, she squealed with delight. At the sound of her laughter, the children came running out and poor Kanzo had to spin each one. Even Saira and Ruby had to have a turn. Kanzo insisted. Neve surprised Ava the most, with the huge smile and spontaneous laughter escaping the grumpy tween.

"When I grow up, will I be as strong as you, Uncle Kanzo?" Tommy asked.

"Of course, as long as you work hard at your skills." Kanzo knelt to grasp the boy on his shoulder. "But a good male must be strong here." He pressed his fingers over his heart.

"Why is your skin a funny color, Uncle Kanzo?" Mikey asked, not willing to let younger Tommy outshine him.

Ava smiled, their competitive streak would come in handy. She had no doubts that the Etterians could handle it.

"I am an Etterian male from the planet Etteria."

"You're an alien?" Neve gasped then did an unexpected thing. She danced with joy. "Way to go, Angel."

"Thank you, I think," Ava said, then kissed Olivia on the cheek. "I must go now to drop Kanzo off before the picnic. We'll see you around nine tomorrow morning."

"We are leaving? It is time?" Kanzo grinned with excitement rolling off him.

She frowned at him, narrowing her eyes as she analyzed his body language. "Yes, but why are you so excited?" Her eyes widened. "You know?"

"What should I know, my Dar Eth?" The way he was smiling at her made butterflies explode in her stomach. She didn't know what his expression meant. But when he looked at her like that, she felt...loved. Her breath hitched. Clearing her throat, she said, "Never mind. Mich was explicit that I drop you off at the bakery."

"It is not necessary." He grinned and kissed her, allowing his tongue to claim her for the briefest of tastes. "I count the seconds before I can claim you again," he whispered then faced Olivia. "I am pleased to have met you, Lady Olivia." He flashed the children a bright smile before whispering into his wrist and phasing out.

"That was awesome," Tommy said, jumping up and down before throwing his arms around Ava's legs.

"Lady?" Olivia asked, a fresh blush blooming.

"Females must be protected," Ava mimicked in a deep voice, failing to sound like an Etterian male, but she didn't care.

"Are all their males like Kanzo?" Olivia asked, her eyes filling with hope.

Ava grinned, after all, Olivia was only thirty-two and certainly allowed to find happiness of her own.

"Yes, and wait till you hear the best part." Ava leaned in to whisper, with Saira and Ruby crowding her, "They mate for life."

Chapter Twenty-Nine

Earth

In the center of town

The Bridal Boutique

"WHAT DO YOU MEAN we're going to try on wedding dresses? Did Mich propose?" Jack asked as Ava climbed into the back of Fred's car.

Squeezed in between Vicky and Taylor, she sat there with unrestrained excitement. No matter how she tried, she couldn't remove the smile from her face. Kanzo had saved her, had saved the orphanage...her Kanzo. Not that she knew what awaited the children, but the fact that they would be fed, looked after, educated, how could she see this in a negative light? Sure, the girls might find Eths, and the boys trained as warriors, but that was a far cry better than life here on Earth.

And now she would be trying on wedding dresses with her sisters. Could this day get any better? But of course, obstinate Jack questioned everything.

"I insisted since I won't get to walk all of you down the aisle." Fred twisted to speak to them. As soon as they'd buckled their seatbelts, he faced forward and drove to the bridal shop. "Please, Jackie, do this for me. I want to see each of you as you might have looked on your wedding day."

At Fred's heartfelt plea, even Ava's eyes misted. She loved this man, her surrogate father. A glance revealed they all did. Fred was pretty special to each of them.

"Okay, Fred, for you," At Jack's capitulation, Ava released a silent sigh of relief. Getting Jack to participate was the biggest hurdle.

"Antoine will meet us at the park with the picnic hampers." Vicky beamed. "I don't know about you, but I could do with a bite of cheesecake."

"Apple pie for me." Ava hummed. "Drowning in tons of cream."

"Mich and the guys will be there as well," Taylor said. "Where is Ulriq? I thought he was with you?"

"We dropped him off at my house on the way here." Jack's blush caused the three of them to laugh.

Ava's smile had once again taken up residence. She cupped her face. Kanzo had said he liked it when she blushed. Perhaps she should ask Der to give him a brain scan, just in case. She chuckled at that thought.

"Wouldn't it be funny if we arrived in our wedding dresses?" Ava said, imagining Kanzo's expression when he saw her in a white gown. The look Jack gave her could've frozen fire. She didn't let it bother her. She was too excited about her life to worry about Jack's temper.

"No, it would not," Jack snapped.

"Jack." Fred met Ava's gaze in the rearview mirror. "Ava, ignore grumpy Jack, of course you can wear your wedding dress to the park."

Ava winked at him in the mirror and squeezed his shoulder.

"I'll wear mine too," Vicky said, before giving Jack a pointed look.

"Let's find dresses first before we decide if we're wearing them out or not." Jack winced, then stretched back to hug Ava in apology.

"We are here," Taylor squealed as she jumped out before Fred had stopped the car.

"Seriously, did Mich propose?" Jack asked as they watched Taylor rush into the bridal store. Then the most remarkable thing happened... Jack paused to admire the dress in the window. Ava almost danced with excitement.

"I think you should try this one on first." She wrapped an arm around Jack's waist before ushering her through the ornate doors.

"Did you say four weddings?" the poor sales assistant whispered, her eyes large in her ashen face.

She ushered over a few more assistants, and soon Ava was in the changing rooms trying on a wedding gown. As she admired the white satin on her lithe figure, she tried to tell herself that this was just a costume, a pretense to get Jack to the altar. But her heart refused to listen. It pounded in her chest, threatening to escape at the first opportunity.

She shouldn't wonder what Kanzo would think of her in a gown since he didn't understand the significance of it. But it was exhilarating to imagine how he would react.

As wonderful as when he'd barged into the Ambassador's chambers and seen her so exposed? As when he'd removed the skirt from her body and couldn't resist kissing her bare stomach?

"Earth to Ava." Vicky poked her head into her booth. "Found anything yet?"

Caught daydreaming, Ava blushed then gestured to the last of the three dresses she'd wanted to try on. "One more, Vicky, then I'll show you." She stepped out of the bulky ballroom gown she'd selected.

"You better, because I need your help. The one I love seems a bit too…" At Vicky's pink cheeks, Ava laughed.

She stepped into the last gown. As the white lace slid over her body, she knew…this was the one. Ava stroked the creases out on her hips, blinking at her reflection. Even though it was too snug, it was exquisite on her. The dress had a high-collared scooped front and lace open-back, dropping to just below her hips, too low for panties, but she didn't care. The mermaid style suited her body, making her appear taller. The soft fabric clung to her curves, and the lace whispered as she moved. She twisted her hair up, pinning it to the top of her head with a few pins the shop assistant held out for her.

"Damn, Ava. You look stunning." Vicky gaped.

"I agree." She twisted from side-to-side. "It's a beautiful gown."

"Beautiful? You make it look incredible. High-collared in lace?" Vicky's expression was skeptical. "I would look like a frump in that. It's your long legs, I tell you."

Ava grinned and ushered Vicky out of her changing room. "Where's your dress? Go try it on while I check on Jack."

She rushed back to the main floor and walked in on Jack standing on the dais, staring at herself in the full-length mirror. She was in the dress from the window's display. It had a sweetheart neckline with spaghetti straps. The pale pink gown fitted her curves snugly to mid-thigh before flaring out. Ava gasped, with the back of the dress a little bare, it somehow softened Jack, making her appear feminine and exquisite. The dress also had sequins and pearls sewn into the bodice with tulle in the flare. If anyone had told Ava she would see Jack in pearls and tulle, she might have had that person committed. Especially when she had never seen Jack in anything other than pants.

"Shit, Jack, I think you found your dress…" Taylor paused on her way past, a few dresses thrown over her arm.

Ava nodded, dumbstruck at how beautiful Jack looked.

"You look amazing, Jackie," Fred said from where he sat on the couch.

"I don't think I'll be having my wedding day, Fred," Jack said as Fred rose to hug her. "I love him and don't need the whole bride thing. The Ethera is far more precious to me."

"He adores you too." Ava glided over to them.

"Ava, is this the one?" Jack asked, wiping away a tear.

Ava beamed, pleased with the dress and with the surprise Ulriq had planned for Jack. "How many did you try on?"

"Only two." She shrugged and stepped onto the dais to stand next to Jack and in front of the full-length mirror. She slipped behind Jack, gathered her curls, and held it on top of her head. They admired the image then laughed. "Okay, maybe leave it down."

"Ulriq likes it down, anyway," Jack said.

"Now, let's check in on Taylor and Vicky." Ava waved as she rushed off. She encountered Taylor first, who'd stepped out of her booth in a pale-blue gown with a sweetheart neckline and the fabric spiraling around her body to the floor, hugging her figure. "Blue? It looks perfect on you." The shop assistant smiled from where she stood just behind Taylor.

"I know, right? I wouldn't have had the courage had you not shown me Lagoon blue." Taylor hugged Ava. "And you look gorgeous, Ava. I've never seen you this perfect. This dress is even better than your Billy-gown. Or maybe it's that twinkle in your eyes... I think I'll call it your Kanzo-sparkle," Taylor teased, giving her a squeeze before releasing her.

"Go show Jack and Fred, Taylor. And I love you too." Ava smiled as she ushered Taylor in Jack's direction before turning to find Vicky.

"Will he like it?" Vicky asked as she stepped from the booth. Her hands twitched at her sides, rising now and then to pinch the fabric.

Ava froze, stunned and delighted at the vision before her. Her throat burned with unshed tears. "Like it? Teric will *love* it." She crossed as fast as the tight dress would allow and grabbed Vicky's hands to tug her toward Fred. She gestured to her to wait as she approached Jack and Taylor giggling like virgin brides.

"So, it's just Vicky now?" Jack asked.

"Yes, she can't choose though." Ava rushed over to stand next to them, barefoot and bouncing on her toes in excitement. "This is the one, watch..." She gestured to the archway where Vicky waited for her signal.

She wore an off-white gown, with a bateau bodice in a sheer fabric and lace detailing. From her cinched-in waist, yards of fabric flared out, ballroom-style to brush along the floor. It looked simple in design until she strode toward them. The yards of fabric parted to reveal her bare leg, all the way to her upper thigh.

"Holy shit, Vicky." Taylor gasped

Vicky's beauty was mesmerizing. Ava sniffed and wiped her eyes. She sneaked a glance at her sisters and flashed a wobbly smile. She wanted to remember this moment forever.

"Stunning." Jack shook her head. "Teric's going to—"

"I know, right?" Vicky giggled, winking at Ava. "I was nervous, after all, I've never worn something this provocative."

"Is this the one?" Taylor asked, hope on her face.

Vicky nodded, and the four women embraced then dragged Fred into their circle. There were tears and laughter all around.

"Do any of you need alterations?" Fred asked, a suspicion of moisture in his eyes.

"Even if we did, there isn't time," Taylor said.

"Mine could be tighter." Vicky spun to show the small pins holding the dress on.

"We can make the alterations within the hour," the assistant said and led Vicky away.

"Ava?" Taylor turned, her gaze traveling over Ava's too-tight gown.

Ava smirked, suspecting that all their evenings had taken a decidedly sexual turn. "Mine's too tight, but with this style, I can get away with it. Jack?" She glanced at Jack, a smile breaking out at seeing her so soft and feminine.

"Mine is perfect," Jack sighed.

"Excellent, now shoes," Fred clapped.

Two and a half hours later, four dressed brides sashayed out of the shop.

"Oh, look. There's a wedding happening in the park," Ava pointed as Fred parked the car. She couldn't wait to see Jack's face, Ulriq's face too, come to think of it.

"I think we best avoid it, Ava. If I was the bride, I'd hate if four strange brides spoiled my day." Vicky winced.

"Not if those brides were my sisters," Taylor said as she peeled herself out of the car.

Ava grinned at how flat-footed Taylor walked, unfamiliar with high heels.

"Wouldn't that be awesome? If we married at the same time?" Vicky stepped forward, exposing a surprisingly well-muscled leg for a chef. And with her dainty transparent slippers, she looked like a princess, a Cinderella out of her comfort zone.

"Too late for that, Vicky. We're already married." Jack flashed a smile and followed behind her as she strolled along a paved pathway leading into the forest.

"Are we there yet?" Taylor said from the back five minutes later. "As pretty as these shoes are, they're killer on the toes."

"The pain of beauty, babe," Ava teased as she trailed Jack.

"I have to admit, it looks strange from my vantage point." Fred chuckled. "I'm the Pied Piper ushering brides away from their grooms."

Taylor groaned. "Well, next time, you can wear the shoes."

"Hell, no, sweetheart." Fred barked out a laugh. "They don't make them in my size."

Vicky stepped aside to let Jack pass, pretending to fix her shoe. She winked at Taylor and Ava, excitement making her hop in place. Not that Taylor was paying them any attention because Michel stood before Jack wearing a charcoal gray tuxedo. Jack and Mich whispered to each other, and it looked like she'd bought the ruse. Mich led Jack further down the path. Ava picked up her hem, slipped off her shoes, and scurried down another path to meet up with Michel at the 'altar.' Whispering fabric meant Taylor and Vicky followed her.

Ava burst into the clearing first and faltered. Kanzo stood there in a matching charcoal gray tux with a pink lily on his lapel. She'd never seen any man look so good like he had stepped off a men's digi-mag. Her mouth dropped open, and she blinked at him, her gaze not sure what to focus on. Taylor nudged her, to remind her that they were on a mission. Caught staring, Ava dipped her chin to hide her flushed face. She rushed over to him, pausing to meet his potent gaze made bluer by his tux.

"Maker, if I thought Vlax's garment was beautiful on you, this...this is mesmerizing," Kanzo said, his voice a hoarse whisper. His gaze traveled over her made-up face, lingering for the longest moment on her lips. "You take my breath away, Ava. Always."

She blushed again at the intensity in his eyes. But at the sound of Jack's approaching voice, she leaned against Kanzo's body and lifted her hem to slide her shoes on. Damn, if she didn't love these shoes. They were white peep-toe stilettos with metal heels and lace inserts. They gave her at least two inches of extra height.

"What are those?" Kanzo growled.

She flashed him a sensual smile in reply and dropped her hem to focus on Jack.

"How private do we need to be?" Jack grumbled.

When they stepped into the clearing, Ava grinned at her ornery friend. She peeked at Ulriq then at Jack, hoping she hadn't missed her surprised expression.

"Here is fine." Michel smiled. "She's all yours, Ulriq."

Jack's head shot up since her attention had been on the path and her complaining. Ava cupped her mouth to muffle a giggle at the sight of her sister lost for words. And the surprise, delight, and pure happiness on her features were so worth it. Ava clung to his arm he slipped around her waist, his fingers splayed across her stomach. Mich kissed Jack on her temple and spun her to face Ulriq, also in a tuxedo, waiting for her beside a pastor.

"What's going on?" Jack's eyes widened.

"It's your wedding, Jack." Mich gestured to Ulriq who waited for her.

Ava glanced at Ulriq, taking the time to admire the big guy in his tux. She smiled at the adoration for Jack on his face.

She squeezed Kanzo's arm, finding the moment made perfect by his presence. It was Jack's figure crossing her vision that brought her back to reality. Not that she had sought her sanctuary, not now and not once since Kanzo had rescued her. With a start, she realized she'd never need her sanctuary again. She glanced at Kanzo, meeting his gaze, blushing at the realization that his attention was on her and not on the wedding. Her gaze traveled over his face, and a sense of peace descended upon her. He would always catch her, no matter what life brought her...them.

He wrapped his other arm around her, pulling her snug against his warmth. She tilted her head to rest her temple on his shoulder, pressing her hand to his hard chest. She toyed with a button on his crisp white shirt. Her whole focus was so on him, on her irregular breathing, on the scent of him, on the feel of his hand at her waist that she missed Jack's words to Ulriq. Then they kissed, the wedding complete with Fred crossing to kiss Jack. Mich did the same. Embarrassed by her inability to focus, Ava stepped away from Kanzo to congratulate the bride.

"I'm sorry, Jack. I almost ruined it with my excitement." She hugged her friend, stepping back to lace her fingers with Kanzo. Being with him was more exciting than having her own wedding day.

"You are so forgiven, all of you." Jack laughed, the brightness of happiness enhancing her lovely features. "I had no idea, not a clue."

"What happens now?" Kanzo asked Ava, whispering in her ear.

She smiled at him, her gaze traversing her face before she blushed and glanced away. "Usually there is a celebratory dinner, but Ulriq wouldn't allow a delay." Ava tried to restrain the shiver that trailed down her back where Kanzo caressed her bared spine with unknown shapes.

"Neither would I." His voice was hoarse as he tightened the hand clasping her hip. "It would kill me to have to wait. It is killing me now." He used their laced fingers to keep her against him.

Her gaze rose to meet his, and she moaned at the mirrored need in his hooded eyes. Tingles scoured a path down her throat to harden her nipples.

"There is protocol we need to follow, Kanzo," she said. He grumbled at her, not pleased to hear this. Ava chose the word protocol knowing he'd understand. "We have to wait for the couple to leave before we can."

Kanzo's gaze flew to where Ulriq stood. Ava's did too. She was grateful that Ulriq planned to leave soon. He lifted Aala into his arms for her to hug him. Then as soon as he lowered her to the ground, he gestured to his O.D.I., and Teric nodded, tugging Aala and Vicky away. Ulriq and Jack phased out, and it appeared as if Ulriq was kissing the hell of Jack, but Ava couldn't be certain. Fred conversed with Taylor and Mich, excitement in his wild gestures, showing no signs he was ready to depart, not yet.

Mich glanced up, spotted Ava and Kanzo, then extricated himself from Taylor's arms. He bounded over and tore Ava out of Kanzo's embrace to hug her.

"What did I say, Angel? Everything will be all right," he said into her ear, while he ran his hand up and down her back. Ava rested her chin on Mich's shoulder but caught Kanzo's frown deepening. He knew Mich wasn't a threat, but she suspected he didn't like her being in another male's arms. "Here, use Taylor's." He shoved something into Ava's hand.

"But...?" Ava pulled away, the weight of car keys in her hand.

"We'll port to the ship and meet you at Olivia's tomorrow morning." Mich offered Kanzo his hand which he accepted, shaking it three times. "Thank you for what you did for the children, Kanzo." Mich laughed. "Who would've thought the male who rescued me would marry one of my sisters. I couldn't be happier, Kanzo. Welcome to the family, brother." Then Mich hugged a startled Kanzo before returning to Taylor's side.

"Brother?" Kanzo stiffened.

"He thinks of you as his brother-in-law." Ava grinned, dangling keys from her finger. "Want to go now?" She stared at him, at his wide smile and the excitement glowing in his eyes.

"Please," he said with a slight tremor in his voice.

Chapter Thirty

Kanzo was quiet as they rode in Vicky's ground vehicle. It wasn't an unpleasant experience, and Ava handled the craft well. Not that he couldn't stop looking at her. He'd turned in his too-small seat to watch her. Her curls caressed her nape, dancing whenever she moved. He twirled one around a finger, reveling in its silky texture. Her smile curled her unnaturally red mouth. His breath hitched at the sight of them. Maker. That color could enhance her attraction. Was it permanent like her tattoo? She switched off the vehicle in front of a housing structure he assumed belonged to her.

"Welcome to my old home," she said and exited the vehicle, circling to open the door for him.

He climbed out, struggling to move in this restrictive tux. Although, he'd endure the torture again if he garnered the same reaction from her. She'd stared at him, her gaze traveling his body like a caress. He hardened in memory of the heat in her eyes and the way her crimson lips had parted.

He looped an arm around her and spun her to pin her against the vehicle. He sipped from her lips, scenting the artificial color. Sliding his hands across her fabric-encased curves, his slipping control tore through him. He wanted to carry her inside, to spread her on her bed, and peel this incredible garment off her body...with his teeth.

"Come, Kanzo, let's go inside." She rested her fingers on his upper arms.

He grunted and allowed her to slip past him. Adjusting his arousal in the constricting pants, he trailed her. Inside the housing unit, he drew in a deep breath, filling his lungs.

"It scents of you." He tugged her into his arms. "Tell me, *thamani*, why do they call you Angel?" He brushed his mouth over hers and shuddered when her tongue teased him. "I know why I would call you such, azula."

"It's just a nickname." She looped her arms around his neck. "Tell me, my Eth, why didn't you mention you were attending the wedding? And who helped you with your tux?" She glanced at his chest, her admiration apparent in her hooded gaze. His arms tightened reflexively.

"I wanted to surprise you. Ulriq commanded I request your assistance with this garment. Mich assisted instead."

"It was a wonderful surprise." She pulled away and turned her back on him. His fingers twitched with the need to stroke her soft, bare skin.

She climbed the stairs. The way her backside swayed, the light reflecting off her skin, glimpses of her calves and her feet in that footwear, left him still standing at the bottom of the stairs gripping the railing.

"Kanzo?"

"Where are you going?" he asked, his voice rough as he lifted his gaze to meet hers.

"To my room. These shoes are killing me."

"They are?" He studied the adored footwear. Was it the metal heels? Could they harm her? Her chuckle made him smile. She teased him, his Dar Eth.

"No, it just feels like it." By now, she'd reached the landing and disappeared from his view.

Not pleased with this, he bounded up the steps, following his nose until he walked into a room. Here her scent was the strongest. The room was in grays and pale blues, the color combination pleasing. His focus returned to her seated on the side of her bed, with the edge of her dress resting on her knees, exposing her calves to his hungry gaze. She had one footwear in hand while she rubbed her toes.

He crossed to her and knelt to grasp her foot. His large fingers massaged the ball and arch, but his gaze never left her face. She moaned, her eyelids fluttered, hiding her thoughts from him. His touch must've been good because her shoe slipped from her fingers. Once done, he rested her foot on his chest, just above his heart before reaching for her other foot. He removed the footwear and massaged her. Her breath caught, and she leaned onto her elbows, her head falling back as pleasure crossed her face.

"You have talented fingers," she rasped.

He stopped. Her head shot up, her brow furrowing in concern.

He blinked at the black curls at the juncture of her thighs, the Ethera driving him hard. Her dress had slipped from her knees to pool across her hips, exposing her feminine folds to his hungry gaze. With a growl, he clasped a foot in each hand and opened his arms wide, guiding her legs to part, revealing the deep pink of her core. A more beautiful image he'd never seen. He groaned and slid his hands along her inner calves, keeping her legs parted, to her inner thighs until he cupped her. He dipped his head and inhaled, slow and deep, his nose brushing her curls. He rumbled his approval.

One thumb he dragged over her seam, while another, he slipped down to hook into her channel. She was so wet...

"You are ready for me, *thamani*." He glanced at her hooded green eyes. "This pleases me." His focus returned to her pink folds. He stroked her seam, dipping in to twirl around her nub, his pace slow. Her hips rose as if begging him to claim her, but he had other plans.

From the moment she'd burst into the clearing at the human ceremony then revealed her strange yet incredible footwear, only one thought reached through his lust-filled mind. To claim her. The realization soon followed. She couldn't wear undergarments in such a curve-hugging garment, and she had stood in his arms with her channel accessible. That he could lift her garment and claim her consumed his mind. It drove him now.

With a guttural groan, he latched his lips over her nub and sucked, growling in the back of his throat at her flavor, at her responses. He worked on her without mercy. If he kept this up, she would find fulfillment soon. He needed her to. The urge to plunge into her was growing impossible to control. Withdrawing his thumb from her channel, he slid in his middle finger, pumping in and out as lashed his tongue across her nub. He leaned back to watch her writhe under his ministrations.

Grinning, he twisted his hand, palm upwards, and froze. Something had an odd texture deep inside her. He toyed and stroked it with his fingertip. She arched off the bed, crying out, her nipples pebbling in reaction. He rubbed it with more vigor, and she writhed, panting his name, shivering with need.

"What is that, azula?" he asked. Her need peaking raised his, as well. His aching arousal throbbed in these too-tight pants he wore.

"G-spot." She shivered as he tormented her further. "Explain later," she said on a whimper.

With a grin, he stroked this G-spot again and sucked on her nub at the same time. With a scream, she twitched, writhed, her nails digging into the linen. His name tumbled from her, and her knees trembled. Her pulse beat along his finger still inside her.

Leaping to his feet, he ripped off his pants and tossed his jacket and shirt aside until he stood there in his footwear. He didn't have the patience to remove them, not with his arousal demanding relief. He slid two hands under her backside to lift her hips off the bed while he knelt. Then in one thrust, he plunged to the hilt. His hard length in her danced black spots across his vision. He growled his pleasure.

He withdrew and thrust in. She found her fulfillment again. The wet heat of her desire flooded his arousal, and her pulsating channel cast him over the edge with her. He roared his release, the sharp tingles flowing straight from his balls to the tip of his malehood with too pleasurable a force. His body shuddered, his breathing came out in gasps, his heartbeat stuttered, and his chest swelled with all the emotion she invoked.

He gathered her near and pinned her against his chest. This way he got to hold her without smothering her. Her sigh was one of contentment when she rested her head on his chest and wrapped her arms and legs around his body as if she too needed him near. Still holding her, he stood and circled her bed to lie on his right side. He tucked her into the curve of his body, her back against his chest, so close a Maloidian dagger couldn't fit between them. Nuzzling her neck and ear, he traced her patterned thigh...tattoo, she'd called it.

"Ava, would you like a wedding day?" he asked into her hair.

She stiffened and twisted to glance over her shoulder at him, a sweet smile warming her eyes. He watched her expression but found no shadows, just joy.

"No, thank you, Kanzo. It's thoughtful of you to ask me, though." She faced away from him and snuggled her backside against his thighs. "I have you, and that's more than enough for me."

His breath hitched, and he tightened his arm. Somehow, being inside her or crushing her to him was never enough to assuage this craving to have her near. He hardened—his malehood physical evidence of how he felt about her.

"*Thamani*, when you say such things to me...it makes me ...hard," he said, his gruff voice no longer his to control. He pressed the evidence of his arousal against her backside, so she wouldn't doubt him.

With a husky chuckle, she rolled over to kiss his chin.

"Show me." She laughed when he *rose* to the challenge.

He flipped her onto her back and spread her thighs faster than he could arm a blaster. With his tip at her entrance, he paused to lose himself in her green eyes, drowning in the heart-stopping affection he saw there.

"*Ensa ra ensa*," he whispered, and with a light kiss on her swollen lips, he slowed his caresses, his thrusting, keeping her gaze burning into his. He showed her how much she meant to him, what words couldn't convey.

Chapter Thirty-One

Etterian Battleship, Kushin
Orbiting Earth
Various Quarters

"Hello." A small voice startled Nerx. He glanced down and frowned at the short human female staring up at him with her huge blue eyes. She was so thin, and she clutched something filthy in her tiny hand. It looked like dirty brown fur from a kreso and appeared to be missing an eye. He frowned at her scarred arms.

"Hello, *minus susa*." He softened his voice to not frighten her.

"Are you the captain?" she asked, her manner bold.

He smiled, liking her courage, her fire. "Captain?" He frowned, waiting for the O.D.I. to update him on her word choice.

"Uncle Kanzo says this is a large ship, and a ship has to have a captain." At her announcement, she gave him a firm nod.

Nerx drew in a deep breath. He didn't have the time nor the inclination to explain the Etterian rankings to an uneducated human female *damu*.

"Yes, I am the captain." He cringed at the lie, although, since he was the acting 'captain,' he wasn't speaking an untruth. Then against his better judgment, he continued, "I am called a Sub-Commander."

She studied him for a moment then raised a hand. "Up."

He scowled at her demand and glanced around, in search of someone to remove her from his presence.

"Up," she said again.

Her eyes darkened with fear, and her shoulders curled in. She gripped the kre-so-fur to her body while sidling closer to his leg.

Something inside him tilted, and he found himself scooping her into his arms. She was small and so light he could hold her against his chest with one arm, which he did, just under her backside. She snuggled against him and rested her tiny head just above his collarbone.

He felt it then...trust. The level of trust she had in him, a stranger, was awe-inspiring. She expected him not to drop her, but also to keep her safe. With her in his arms, he instructed his males as they remodeled a few officer quarters to suit the needs of the human offspring. He kept his jaw on the crown of her head, to ensure she was secure in his arms and realized he found her sweet scent pleasant. Her presence comforted him.

Her breathing grew calmer, and her hand slipped and rested in her lap, implying she'd fallen asleep. Yet nothing drove him to put her down, to locate someone to see to her needs. He continued to hold her, to enjoy the trust of a *damu*. His males respected him, but that he'd earned. This *damu* trusted him on faith.

"She naps for about an hour, then she'll be energized again." A human female smiled at him. He blinked at her exquisite purple eyes, having never seen eyes that color. "I'm Olivia..."

He spun on the spot, expecting her to follow him. She did so with a chuckle.

"Welcome, Lady Olivia." He gestured to the quarters. "Please take a moment and assess if this would suit your needs?" He activated a door and waited for her to enter the main room.

A bed rested against the left wall, large enough for an Etterian male. On the other side, there were a few comfys at a lower height to accommodate the *damu*, and he'd added a few more display vids to the walls.

"The replicators and rehydrators have restricted access, as do the access panels for all the doors. We lowered the waste receptacles and stocked the cleansing rooms with smaller wraps. The water cleanses everything so no soap is required. We lowered the beds, as well. A male will guard each quarters as an additional precaution. You need to vet the males selected."

"That is wonderful, Nerx. Your males seem to have a calming effect on the children. I appreciate their willingness to guard them for me." She flashed him another smile. That she didn't address him by his title had him grumbling, but he couldn't expect her to follow protocol when she knew it not.

"Your quarters are across the passage, with the ladies Ruby, Neve, and Saira sharing quarters as requested. Theirs is alongside yours for convenience."

"Is there closet space, Nerx?" Olivia asked as she entered a bedroom.

He touched a metallic panel—it opened to reveal shelves and hooks. His males had lowered them for easier access.

"How...?" Olivia spun in a circle. "How is this possible?"

"The bulkheads are modular and depending on the design, can clip and lock into position. The waste receptacles had to be custom replicated, but other than that, the adjustments were simple enough."

"Thank you for explaining and for going to all this effort. I'm happy and grateful." Olivia glanced at him and rubbed the sleeping *damu*'s back. "Need me to take her from you?"

He hesitated. Something within him refused to relinquish the *damu*.

Olivia's eyes widened then she nodded, dropping her hand.

"May I keep her for now?" he asked.

"Yes, although, she may pee on you," Olivia said.

His eyelids fluttered while his O.D.I. rushed to update him on the word 'pee.' Shock gripped him, and he fought the urge to yank the *damu* off his chest.

"She used to when she first came to me. Scarred and scared, the slightest noise would cause her to wet herself." Olivia's smile was bright despite the dour subject matter. "Relax, Nerx, I was kidding. She'll let you know when she needs to go."

"Who harmed her?" He didn't like the scars marking her body.

"Her father, so the fact that Lily trusts you and Kanzo is a miracle in itself." And on that note, Olivia left him to wander the rooms.

Nerx rubbed Lily's back. If he had the father's name, the battleship would make one illegal stop. And start a war with Earth in the process? He scowled. Perhaps just a shuttle trip to the surface might be better received.

He went about his duties, ignoring the stares from his males, keeping his voice to a softer level, though just as fierce lest his males question his authority.

"Do you want me to take Lily?" Ava asked as she approached him.

He stood on the upper platform of the bay, watching his males perform their tasks. "I am permitted to keep her with me for now."

She shrugged. "Don't tell the other children, but she's my favorite." Her tone was conspiratorial.

Nerx agreed with her assessment.

"Trust Lily to find the biggest and baddest alien and make him her champion," a human female, halfway to fully grown, giggled at the sight of Lily in his arms.

"That is an untruth." He scowled.

"Neve means that Lily found the strongest and fiercest Etterian male to protect her," Ava said.

Nerx forced a stiff smile to indicate he understood the female youngin's intention. "Then it is a truth."

Ava sighed then dug in a bag. She unwrapped what she had found and held it up to him. "Here, eat this," she said.

Her tone was so commanding, he opened his mouth only to scowl when chocolate coated his tongue. "I do not need..."

She ignored him and shoved the remaining re-wrapped chocolate bar in his back pocket. He glared at her and jerked out of her reach, not appreciating her taking liberties with his person.

"Give the chocolate to Lily when she wakes up." She spun on her heels, gathered a few black rectangular boxes, and ushered Neve down the passage.

He grumbled as he finished the chocolate she'd shoved in his mouth, only admitting to himself he had needed it.

Chapter Thirty-Two

Etterian Battleship, Kushin
En route to Etteria
Kanzo's Quarters

"Warrior Kanzo," Adviser Cales greeted him as soon as Kanzo accepted the communication request. "The King has reviewed your unusual application. He has granted his approval. I, however, am pleased to hear your Dar Eth has such a skill. Please enquire whether she would be willing to perform the Foot of Honor?" At Cales's question, Kanzo's eyes widened. He hadn't considered that Ava could provide such a service to Etteria.

"I will discuss this with her, though she may need to test her skill. Our hair is far different from human hair. And her other requirements?"

Adviser Cales grinned. According to the buzz, he disliked cutting hair, hence his open joy. "Our engineers have located a suitable chamber and are in the process of modifying it as per their research. As soon as you have discussed my suggestion, and hopefully, Lady Ava agrees, I will instruct them to consider assisting her with the Foot of Honor. Her equipment might need modifications for such a task."

"A wise consideration, Adviser," Kanzo smiled.

"Congratulations on finding your Dar Eth, Kanzo. Lenzo would have been annoyingly arrogant about it."

"You knew my father?" Kanzo arched a brow with delighted surprise.

"Of course, an honorable male amongst males."

"Thank you, Adviser Cales, for attending to my request." And the vid went black from Cales's side. One did not end a comm on such a high-ranked male—it was disrespectful.

Kanzo chuckled. Not only had he petitioned the king, but he hoped to be able to assist Adviser Cales. He prayed his efforts pleased Ava. That was all that mattered to him.

Planet Etteria
Royal City of Issneen
Off the Royal Gardens

"Kanzo, how far do you plan on leading me?" she asked blindfolded as he led her forward a few more steps.

"We are there, *thamani*. You will be most pleased," he said in his deep voice.

She sighed at the sound of it, willing to let him lead her anywhere. He shifted behind her, and with the gentlest of touches, removed the sash covering her eyes. She blinked at the bright pink light of Etteria's sky, then leaned back to smile at him. He gripped her shoulders and faced her forward.

At the sight before her, she gaped. Joy so intense it summoned tears flooded her. A white stone building, so like the others in Issneen, had rounded corners and a slanted roof in gray. Blue grass and pink flowers lined the walkway leading to the door. *Azula's* was etched on the large glass windows reflecting her pale face.

"Will this do?" he asked.

His question and the level of eagerness in his voice amazed her. Would this do? Was he insane to ask such a question? He'd created a salon just for her?

"The king said yes? You asked him?" Her breathless questions he answered with a nod and a dimpled smile.

"Lima Brac awaits you inside to explain how the machinery works."

It hit her then. This was hers, all of it. A gift from Kanzo worth more than he'd ever know. She squealed and threw her arms around him, burying her face into his neck, inhaling the scent she now thought of as home.

"Thank you, thank you, thank you." She peppered kisses along his neck.

"My pleasure, *ensa*." He crushed her to him. She wished she could do more than hug him, something to show him her gratitude. "Adviser Cales asked if you would cut dishonorable males' hair, as well. I informed him that I would discuss it with you first. You might need to practice as well."

She frowned. "I've cut hair for many years."

Kanzo grinned and released his metal tie. Not once had she had a chance to run a comb through his hair. Now, as it unraveled itself from its fishtail braid to swirl around him, she understood why. It was a strange sight. He looked like he was underwater. She stepped forward in amazement to touch his hair and sink her fingers into the silken depths, cool and caressing. Yes, his hair stroked up her arms and entwined with her fingers.

"It likes you," he said, his ice-blue gaze traveling her face. What he read there, she couldn't say.

"Does it hurt if it's cut?" she asked, concerned it might bleed, or the males might need anesthesia. He shook his head. "So, it moves constantly? Like a four-year-old child?"

She glanced at him just as his hair, now wrapped around her arms like thick bracelets, tugged her enough to unbalance her. She stumbled toward him with a gasp. He caught her, but his hair yanked again until she sprawled across his chest.

He laughed. "As I said, it likes you."

"Are all males' hair going to be like this?" she asked with her face pressed against his velvety skin.

"Their hair will attack you," he said. She squeaked in response. "Adviser Cales usually leaves it braided."

"All right. Are there males I can practice on?"

"You can test your skill on me." His statement had her gaze rising to meet his. Was he serious? She knew how much they valued their hair, and for him to offer... A tear formed and slipped out at the sheer enormity of his sacrifice. He would let her near his honor, to cut it off as if she punished him.

"Why would you trust me to do this? To take what doesn't need to be taken?"

He lifted a hand to catch her tear as it slipped free. "I harmed you, *thamani*, when we first met. I wish to make amends."

She shook her arm and the hair loosened enough for her to place her hand on his chest. "You didn't. I misunderstood you. Kanzo, you don't need to make amends. Twice you saved me, saved the children, and organized this for me." She gestured to her salon, still dazed at seeing her nickname on the glass. "You're a wonderful male, Kanzo."

"I am pleased you think so, *thamani*. More than you know. Malia pa," he whispered. She gasped again, as his hair braided itself as if by magic. He caught the end and slipped the clip on. "Maloidian steel is the only thing that calms it."

He ushered her toward the glass door which opened as he neared it. Inside, the walls were white and two seats faced mirrors. Couches in greens and blues dominated one corner, a tiny 'kitchen' sat at the back. Two doors led off, she assumed one was a bathroom. Her gaze settled on an Etterian male, huge, muscled, and in his late forties.

She liked him on sight.

"I'm pleased to meet you, Lima Brac." She held out her hand. He accepted it with a smile, glancing at Kanzo as if to ensure he was holding her hand correctly. He shook it three times. She dipped her chin to hide a smile.

"As I am pleased to meet you, milady. When I received your Eth's strange request, I was inspired to do as much as I could. I am hopeful you will approve of my efforts."

"I'm so grateful for all you've done." She laced Kanzo's fingers with hers, then flashed him a look, trying to convey how much he meant to her. "Let Adviser Cales know it's a yes."

Kanzo's beaming smile was a reward on its own.

Chapter Thirty-Three

THE MAGNUS SUN HAD yet to rise when Kanzo trailed his wonderful Dar Eth as she ran past the unopened market stalls. This morning she wore black leggings and a pink sleeveless tunic she called a 'top.' He sighed, content to run behind her and watch her backside sway, as always. After so many weeks of waking up to her beautiful smile, kissing her whenever he wanted to, and claiming her at least once a day, he was the happiest male on Etteria.

Yet, despite how joyful he was, there was something bothering his Ava. She would open her mouth as if to tell him then blush. Her mouth would snap closed, and she would hurry away from him with her shoulders slumped.

No, this morning, determination drove him. She should know by now his happiness rested upon hers. He caught up to her and gestured northeast of their usual path, and she nodded, following him as he led her to the tidal pools. It was the only place in Issneen that allowed swimming since the pools were free of the carnivorous omeika. These fish were dangerous to catch, prepare, or eat when they had razor-sharp teeth and upon death, their skin released a deadly toxin. Yet it remained one of Etteria's top exports. He paused on the crest of the hill, under the Fuyra statue of an Etterian male, King Xeus's ancestor, Pius, holding a greatsword overlooking the ocean.

"Do you swim?" Kanzo asked, his voice husky with what he planned.

"Swim?" She blessed him with a bright smile while stretching her calf muscles.

"Yes, I feel like a swim in the tidal pools. Interested?" He ran his gaze along the length of her.

She slowed her stretches to trail a seductive hand over her inner thigh. Arching her back, she raised her arms, thrusting her breasts forward.

"I am definitely interested." She rested her gaze for a long period on his arousal.

He loved it when she looked at him like that, caressing him with her eyes. He grabbed her hand and led her down a narrow-hidden path to the carved stone tidal pools rising out of the rocky shore. The deep gray stone was smoothed over many centuries. The water lapped at the sides and the carved steps leading into the pool's depths. He led her to the smaller of the two, not as deep but still sufficient for his intentions.

With a grin, he toed off his sneakers and socks, peeled off his tunic, and dove in. He stood in the water, which was only nipple-high for him, while he waited for her. She undressed under his potent gaze, ripping off her small tunic, then, to his delight, shimmied out of her leggings until she stood before him naked.

"Ava." He grinned. "Someone might see you so…"

She laughed at his teasing. "You have advanced hearing. We'll know before they get here. Besides, it's too early for spectators, and this way, my clothes will be dry for the run back." She dove in, breaking through the red waves in front of him. He pulled her near, loving her water-slicked breasts against his chest. He claimed her mouth, kissing her, trying to show her how much she meant to him, how she made his heart ache with intense emotion.

"Now, tell me, Ava, my *thamani*, what is the matter?" He hugged her, implying he wouldn't release her until she shared her concerns with him.

She clung to him in the cool water, shivering against him. Tiny bumps coated her skin. She raised her gaze to his while touching every part of his body rising above the surface.

"A few days ago, I activated the Etterian Language Protocol in order to speak to the Etterian females who'd volunteered to help with the children. I now know *thamani* means beloved. How many times have you called me *thamani*? For how long now?"

He frowned, not understanding what she was asking him. "You are worrying me, Ava."

"I'm sorry, Kanzo." She stroked her fingers along his jaw to cup his cheek, carrying water rivulets to run down his neck. "I've wasted so much time. I'm such a fool."

"Speak clearly, my Dar Eth. What do you need?" he asked, tightening his hold with one arm to brush damp curls off her temple.

She drew in a deep breath, pressing her breasts against his chest. As a distraction, it was a good one. "I love you, *thamani*."

At her words, warmth wrapped around his heart, altering its rhythm and deepening the peace he felt. "You know how I feel, Ava." He crushed her against him, trapping her within the circle of his arms.

"No, I don't. I don't have your preternatural senses, Kanzo. I need you to tell me."

"Very well." He lowered his hands to grab her backside, yanking her to him so that her legs could wrap around his hips. "I love you, Ava." Her breath caught, and her eyes glistened with unshed tears. Ah, now he understood. "Telling you should make you joyful," he teased while rubbing her bare back.

She laughed. "I am joyful." She snuggled against him. "How long have you known?"

"I knew the moment we met, but I fought it. I did not want you to consume my every thought." He dipped his head to kiss her temple. "I cannot exist without you now, my Dar Eth."

"I fought it too, any excuse not to love you," she said.

"Because of Billy," he said.

She met his gaze and blushed. "How long have you known I loved you?"

"Since you gave your body to me. You do not need to tell me, azula. You do so with every touch."

"So do you. I was just too blind to see." She claimed his mouth with a kiss of her own. She was bold, commanding and so passionate.

He groaned and crushed her to him. "I am sorry too," he said into her mouth. "Had I known you would kiss me like this..."

She chuckled and hugged him tighter.

"Now do you wish you'd removed your shorts?" She pressed an open-mouthed kiss to his neck.

"Alodon's balls, yes."

She pushed herself away from him, paddling to keep herself afloat, her breasts and nipples peeking through the water. "Hurry then," she said, laughing when he removed his shorts and tossed the sodden lump out of the pool. She swam toward him again. He dragged her closer. As soon as her body touched his, she moaned and lifted her legs to wrap around his hips. Doing so also positioned her entrance just over the head of his arousal. He groaned, deep and needy as he thrust upward, impaling her on his length.

"This is why you are my azula. Only a celestial being could make me this happy," he said, his voice hoarse as he plunged into her, angling his hips to bring her to a rapid release, claiming her in a never-ending ocean of pleasure. As his Maker and the Ethera had intended.

GLOSSARY

Etterians worship one God, one Maker, since the universes have only His fingerprint on all of it, a single golden thread through all of creation.

Tokens: intergalactic form of currency

Kliks: predetermined length of distance.

Hatimaye – To bring an end (Hutt-ee-my-ee)

Etterian

Alodon (A-low-donn): who accidentally shot his balls off with his own blaster.

Teacher: lima (lee-ma)

Great teacher: lima kuu: (lee-ma koo)

Directions: semit (semm-it)

Lemon: giyua (gee-you-a)

Young one: damu (daa-moo)

Heart: ensa (enn-sa)

Heart of my heart: ensa ra ensa (enn-sa raa enn-sa)

Beloved: thamani (ta-mar-nee)

Little joy: minus susa (mee-nas soo-sa)

Little cat: minus cesu (mee-nas sess-oo)

Large: magnus (mag-nis)

Orgasm: fulfillment/deite asteri (see stars) / released (day-ta ass-tare-ree)

Starfighter: asteri peju (ass-tare-ree pear-joo)

Collection of glass vials: virak (vee-ruck)

Scum of the galaxies: xemi (ze-mee)

Hair up: malia pa (Mar-lee-a par)

Hair down: malia pado (Mar-lee-a par-dow)

Lysaran

Visitor: kashi (Kaa-shee)

God: Kaiha (Kigh-haa)

King: Kuna (Koo-na)

Orange fleshy fruit: Lemte (Lem-ta)

White flowers: Myameru (My-a-me-roo)

Precious: Delica (Dell-ee-ka)

Sweetheart: Sali (Saa-lee)

Arum Lily-type flower: D'nastu (D-nass-too)

Love Blossom: aroa loulu (A-row-a low-loo)

Maloidian

Title of respect: lommia (Lomm-ee-a)

Stubborn, lethal tree: tewaa (Tee-wah)

Tokauri/Kulai

Blade – Sulac (soo-lack)

Bone – Ukog (you-cog) - bone from some dumb animal, probably an ukog.

Braided – Gisul (gee-sool)

Father – Danno (dan-no)

Heart – Kassu (cass-soo)

Maker – Mugbu (Mug-boo)

Mother – Manno (man-no)

Sapphires – Buha (boo-ha)

Shit – Saho (sa-ho)

Star - stuon (stoo-on)

Stupid – Ungog (oon-gog)

Vessel/ship - sakay (sa-kay)

Pronunciations

Names

Aaro - Ah-row

Adda – Ay-dah

Aldur - Al-durr

Alllero - A-le-row

Balllio – Bah-leee-oh

Bos - Boss

Bry-dar - Brigh-darr

Brynr - Brin-ner

Cales - Cale-es

Cento - Sen-tow

Citus - Sigh-tuss

Coldar - Coal-daar

Cria - Kree-ah

Eriz - Sigh-low

Danic - Dan-eek

Deeezo – Dee-zoh

Der - Durr

Diso - Dee-sow

Diyo - Die-oh

Eira - Eye-raa

Enyl - E-neel

Eriz - E-rizz

Garix - Ga-ricks

Gayn - Gain

Iddan - Ee-dann

Idon - Eye-donn

Illan - Ee-lann

Jarg – Jar-g

Jokta - Jock-tar

Kanzo - Can-zow

Keelu – Key-loo

Keryr – Kerr-eer

Ksal - Ka-sell

Lazu – Lah-zoo

Lurz - Lurr-z

Malo - Mail-oh

Matir - Mat-teer

Myan - My-ann

Myn-ras - Min-russ

Naio – Nay-oh

Nerx - Nurcks

Nuos - New-oss

Oyaz - Oh-yaz

Prex - Precks

Ronin - Row-nin

Saan - Sarn

Sena - See-na

Sy'mar - Sigh-marr

Syna - Sigh-na

Tamra – Tum-rah

Taro - Tah-row

Tenu - Ten-oo

Trav - Trahv

Tinh - Tin

Vytus - Vie-tuss

Vodin - Vo-din

Ulriq - Yule-rick

Vorn - Vawn

Vyar - Vie-arr

Xan - Zan

Xeus – Zeus

Zaro - Zah-row

Ziot - Zye-ott

Places

Argaxx – Are-jax

Crustiiu – Criss-tee-oo

Dyuqa - Dee-you-ka

Etteria – E-tare-rea

Galaza – Gah-Lar-Zah

Gikaet – Gee-ka-ett

Iphara = Ee-far-ra

Kulai – koo-ligh

Lysara – Liss-saa-ra

Mascroba – Mus-crow-ba

Resia Cay – Ress-Ee-ahh Kay

Sarvis – Sarr-viss

Sosu – Sow-soo

Tokauri – Too-cow-ree

Yithia – Yith-ee-a

Battleships

Chikara – Chee-kar-a - Force

Gladio – Glad-ee-oh - Sword

Kushin – Cush-shin - To Pierce

Surata – Soo-ra-tah – Beginning

Usaha – Oo-saa-hah - Endeavor

Shuttles

Celeeri – See-lee-ree - swift

    Denessi – Denn-ess-ee - sodge

    Eshima – Ee-shee-ma - respect

    Kevol – Kev-oll - agony

    Kuta – Koo-tah - modular shuttle.

    Liri-ny – Lee-ree-nye – freedom

    Misaia – Miss-aye-a - memory

    Sasay – Sass-ay - whispers

    Yakin – Yuck-kin - belief

Creatures

Asnu – Ass-Noo – buffalo/donkey

    Eiltur – Ale-turr

    Gracc – Grrr-ack

    Ilag – Ee-Lug– leggy slugs that feast on sol.

    Kreso – Kreh-soo

    Omeika – Oh-may-ka

    Pagsu – Pug-Soo - cocksuckers

    Reshy – Resh-Ee - huge, like the size of a kuta shuttle, with massive jaws and rows of sharp teeth.

    Sogair – Sow-gare

    Wilanegy – Will-anna-jee

About the Author

Sevannah Storm is a fiction writer who immerses herself in fantastical worlds both magical and science fiction. She has a flair for the creative having studied art and interior architecture and spends her time drawing, oil painting, and writing. An avid reader from an early age, Sevannah finds her inspiration from various sources: games, novels, music, and the land of make-believe. The unique versus the practical has brought on numerous debates.

In her spare time, she does Krav Maga, CrossFit, and rereads novels that snatch her breath away. Having embraced the social media world, you can find her on most platforms.

Her home is a land south of Wakanda, where animals roam free. Born in Zimbabwe, she grew up in South Africa. The crisp blue skies with cotton-candy sunsets expand her heart and soul, encapsulating a sense of freedom.

Words she lives by: "Know your pothole and dodge it. Don't work in a pencil factory if you're a vampire."

Sevannah loves to hear from her readers. You can find and connect with her at the links below.

Website/Newsletter:

https://www.sevannahstorm.com/

Facebook:

https://www.facebook.com/sevannah.storm

Instagram:

https://www.instagram.com/sevannah.storm/

Twitter:

https://twitter.com/sevannah_storm

Thank you for taking the time to read Sun Forged. If you enjoyed the story, please tell your friends and leave a review. Reviews support authors and ensure they continue to bring readers books to love and enjoy.

https://sevannahstorm.com

SOUL FORGED

The Gifting Series #1

Know-it-all Oriana agreed to travel with aliens who need women. But she didn't agree to abduction, life/death battles, and escaping with a bossy, arrogant man. She was sabotaged, attacked, and kidnapped, but she is far from beaten. Forced to participate in an alien battle arena with no promise of freedom, she has to forget the loss of her family and focus on surviving.

Enyl has given up hope. His people are dying due to a genetic modification gone awry. Darkness is consuming his warriors, and his world, as he knows it, will end. His father, the king, has rolled out a plan to save them all. But Enyl doubts a solution will be found in time.

And when a compatible female is found...and lost, he must rescue her, a human female capable of surviving despite all odds. However, freeing Oriana serves to anger the aliens holding her captive. Ensuring she is cared for—as per Etterian protocol—he is stunned by the strong connection between the two of them. Such a bond was only experienced between Etterian mates.

Is she his salvation or is that wishful thinking on his part?

Read it here:

https://books2read.com/u/mlAWr9

FATE FORGED

THE GIFTING SERIES #2

Jacqueline (Jack) Dunois struggles to find a man not intimidated by her career as a law enforcement instructor, especially in the small town she calls home. She would sacrifice a kidney to find someone who would make her ovaries clap and didn't live with his mother. Then she meets a supreme commander from another world who thinks the stars in the galaxies shine in her eyes... What's not to love about that?

Supreme Commander Ulriq doesn't believe in love, an archaic term for a volatile and untrustworthy emotion Etterians were no longer subjected to. Until he meets Jack who triggers the Ethera, the soulmate force that irrevocably changes a male when he finds his ideal female. At that moment, his world, his focus, his very loyalty shifts. But when she is taken from him, it is too much to bear. Under the influence of the Ethera, he launches a rescue. He'll start a war and kill anyone who dares stop him, just to have her back in his arms.

Read it here:

https://books2read.com/u/bMY09v

WAR FORGED

The Gifting Series #4

Being kidnapped by aliens does not sit well with Quinlan. Not only would her seven guardians give her hell if she doesn't attempt some sort of escape, but she refuses to be at anybody's mercy. With her practiced military skills, the help of an underground lounge singer and a personal assistant, she takes over the alien slave ship. Not knowing how to fly the damn thing, she sends a distress signal. …The rescue comes swiftly in the form of a bronzed man with exquisite ice-blue eyes. Leaving her to ask the true question: has she just given up her newfound freedom for a gorgeous man who seems determined to have her for eternity?

As Elite Supreme Commander of the Etterian Forces, Xan answers a distress call in Earth English. That is all he did. The female who captured the slave ship shows remarkable skill, making her a warrior in her own right. Said skills should be respected and honored. Except she is his Dar Eth, calling forth the Ethera—the soulmate bond. How can he protect his female when she can do so herself? What can she possibly need from him? What can he offer a female, not Etterian but human? Not that he can think clearly in her presence when she scents so good and makes him want to kiss all of her.

Maker help him.

Read it here:

https://books2read.com/u/bz1QGD

STAR FORGED

SHADOW FORGED

Forty-year-old Caroline is too old to start dating and too bored with her vibrator, but what other choices does she have. On the day she burns her shirt and breaks a fingernail, she meets Etterian warriors. As part of her job at E.S.A. (Earth Space Association,) she must 'entertain' the hot-as-apple-pie Chief Engineer she suspects isn't who he claims to be.

Operations Commander Malo, Head of Espionage, must act as an engineer and ambassador, hoping to invite human females to visit Etteria and save his dying race. From Princess Oriana, he has strict instructions to distrust humans. What he finds he cannot trust are his emotions and his body whenever in the presence of the human ambassador, Caroline. She does not believe in soulmates or in a forever with him. Convincing her to choose him is the greatest task ever set before him, one he cannot afford to fail.

Until she is stolen from him. He calls in favors, utilizes all his resources to find her. And *when* he does, he is never letting her off his battleship...or his bed.

Read it here:

https://books2read.com/u/bPNd8j

"

EARTH FORGED

The Gifting Series #7

Guilt hounds Izzy, who caused her sister's injury and subsequent blindness. But no matter how she cares for Simone or what she sacrifices, it doesn't ease the ache in her chest. With Simone and naive Caro, her best friend, Izzy's role as protector is fully realized. The cost? Hiding behind quirkiness, pseudo-joy, and giving up her hopes and dreams. What she needs is a knight in any armor. After all, beggars can't be fussy. She has no idea that armor, in her case, means black military and that a knight could come in any color, specifically bronze.

Oyaz wants to find his life force, his soulmate, and he'd like her to be human. Earth's females are soft, amusing, passionate, and their scents rival a garden of hahyt blossoms. His task is to guard their planet that promises so many salvations for his males. It's a duty he's pleased to perform, one he would die for. When Operations Commander Malo orders Oyaz to retrieve a human female, he's eager to oblige. That it would lead to his salvation is something he couldn't anticipate. What he hadn't planned for is an ambush that costs him more than his memory, the loss of his soulmate.

Now what? Nothing in their training prepared him for this.

And yet, despite not remembering kneeling for Izzy, he longs to claim her with every inch of his soul.

Read it here:

https://books2read.com/u/31V82D

LUST FORGED

THE GIFTING SERIES #8

Ex-socialite Leona wants nothing more than to enhance the mechanics within sex-cybs, not to mention improve their performances with their 'lovers.' It's a job where she's safe in an all-woman factory on Callisto, and far from her matchmaking mama. When the chief engineer is incapacitated, Leona's required to gift—her term would be pimp—sex-cyborgs to prospective clients. On an Etterian battleship, surrounded by gorgeous males, she tries not to think of sex when it's her work, especially with the Sub-Commander Aaro whose neon-blue eyes are the stuff of her erotic dreams.

As a diplomatic favor, Aaro must abandon his task to guard Earth, and perhaps find his Dar Eth or soulmate, all to protect cargo en route to many worlds, including the dangerous and unpredictable Yithia. Princess Oriana is most concerned for the two human female engineers determined to ensure the deliveries are successful. A simple enough mission until one human enters Aaro's cargo bay, dropping him to his knees.

But revealing to independent Leona that she's now trapped in a marriage isn't something Aaro can bring himself to do. He violates all he stands for, every ounce of honor by not telling her the truth. All in the hopes that she will choose to love him.

Read it here:

https://books2read.com/u/3LdA1w

www.ingramcontent.com/pod-product-compliance
Lightning Source LLC
Chambersburg PA
CBHW070302120726
47910CB00007B/2345